Sweetgrass
Basket

Sweetgrass Basket

by MARLENE CARVELL

DUTTON CHILDREN'S BOOKS

DUTTON CHILDREN'S BOOKS A division of Penguin Young Readers Group Published by
the Penguin Group · Penguin Group (USA) Inc., 375 Hudson Street, New York, New York 10014,
U.S.A. · Penguin Group (Canada), 90 Eglinton Avenue East, Suite 700, Toronto, Ontario, Canada
M4P 2Y3 (a division of Pearson Penguin Canada Inc.) · Penguin Books Ltd, 80 Strand, London
WC2R 0RL, England · Penguin Ireland, 25 St Stephen's Green, Dublin 2, Ireland (a division of
Penguin Books Ltd) · Penguin Group (Australia), 250 Camberwell Road, Camberwell, Victoria 3124,
Australia (a division of Pearson Australia Group Pty Ltd) · Penguin Books India Pvt Ltd, 11 Community
Centre, Panchsheel Park, New Delhi - 110 017, India · Penguin Group (NZ), Cnr Airborne and
Rosedale Roads, Albany, Auckland 1310, New Zealand (a division of Pearson New Zealand Ltd) ·
Penguin Books (South Africa) (Pty) Ltd, 24 Sturdee Avenue, Rosebank, Johannesburg 2196,
South Africa · Penguin Books Ltd, Registered Offices: 80 Strand, London WC2R 0RL, England

Library of Congress Cataloging-in-Publication Data
Carvell, Marlene.
Sweetgrass basket / by Marlene Carvell.
p.   cm.
Summary: In alternating passages, two Mohawk sisters describe their lives at the Carlisle Indian
Industrial School, established in 1879 to educate Native Americans, as they try to assimilate into
white culture and one of them is falsely accused of stealing.
ISBN 0-525-47547-8
1. United States Indian School (Carlisle, Pa.)—Juvenile fiction.   [1. United States
Indian School (Carlisle, Pa.)—Fiction.   2. Sisters—Fiction.   3. Identity—Fiction.
4. Mohawk Indians—Fiction.   5. Indians of North America—New York (State)—Fiction.
6. Boarding schools—Fiction.   7. Schools—Fiction.   8. Pennsylvania—History—1865—Fiction.]
I. Title.
PZ7.C2535Sw 2005
[Fic]—dc22   2004024374

Published in the United States by Dutton Children's Books,
a division of Penguin Young Readers Group
345 Hudson Street, New York, New York 10014
www.penguin.com/youngreaders

Designed by Irene Vandervoort   Printed in USA   First Edition
3   5   7   9   10   8   6   4   2

*The author would like to thank Aunt Margaret, although she is
no longer with us, for providing the inspiration; Barbara Landis
and the Cumberland County Historical Society for her advice
and knowledge and the use of their resources; Mary Louise White,
the niece and "adopted" daughter of Aunt Margaret,
for sharing the memories of her own boarding-school experiences;
and my husband, Gerald, for letting his family be mine.*

A NOTE ABOUT Pronunciation

Like most Native American languages, Mohawk is very complex. It does not have a long history as a written language, and so there are variant spellings, and pronunciation is dependent on specific geographic location, generation, etc. There is also some influence and crossover from the other Iroquois tribes. Below are the phonetic pronunciations to the Mohawk words used in *Sweetgrass Basket*:

ake'nistenha	ah-GAY-nees-TUNH-ah
aktsi:'a	ahk-TSEE-ah
Akwesasne	ahg-wah-SAHS-nay
Gai'wiio'	guy-WEE-yo
Haudenosaunee	HOE-d'no-SHOW-nay
he'en	hunh
Kaianerekowa	gah-yah-NAY-le-GO-wah
Kanien'kehaka	gahn-yung-GAY-hah-gah
nia:wen	nee-AH-onh
nia:wenkowa	nee-AH-onh-GO-wah
ontiatshi ne'e	onh-ja-ji-NAY-ay
rake'niha	rah-GAY-nee-ah
satketsko	saht-GETS-go
Tadodaho	dah-doh-DAH-hoe
Waienhawi	wah-yen-HAW-wee

AUTHOR'S NOTE

The Carlisle Indian Industrial School (1879-1918) was the nation's first off-reservation school for Native Americans. When people learn about this school, located in southern Pennsylvania, it is probably the image of Indian children from the western states that comes to mind, as many stories have been written of the Indian boarding-school experiences of the Lakota, Ojibwe, and other children from western and midwestern tribes. Yet, of the over 150 tribes represented at Carlisle, the Mohawks, an eastern tribe which spans the U.S.–Canadian border in upstate New York, and which had already been exposed to European-based culture for over two hundred years, had the sixth largest population at the school, with over 350 children attending Carlisle during its existence. My husband's Mohawk grandfather was one of twelve children. Although he was sent to a school in Montana, of his six siblings who survived past the age of five, two were sent to a school in Buffalo, New York, and four attended Carlisle. The following story is for the thousands of children, at Carlisle and other schools, who found themselves far away from home.

Sweetgrass Basket

saraн

Ake'nistenha

Mother

Were it not for Mattie, I would turn around
and climb up the iron steps and hide in the seats
and hope the train would take me home.

Akwesasne

Home

If my satchel were not so heavy,
I could hold Mattie's hand, but it is filled with the bread
and cakes and early apples Father placed in it for the trip.
If we had been hungry, we would have eaten and
my load would be lighter and I could hold Mattie's hand.

But my stomach swirled back and forth,
back and forth all day with the movement of the train,
and the strong smell of the smoke filled my head,
and I could not eat.

Mattie could not eat either,
but Mattie never eats as much as I do.

"Be good," Father said as he watched us board the train.

Through the window clouded in dust and dew,
I saw his mouth move as he waved good-bye,
but I heard nothing except for the grating
sound of metal against metal as the train
began to move forward.

I wish he had smiled.
I remember when he used to smile.

His figure grew smaller and smaller until
just before he almost faded from view,
I saw him turn and walk away
toward the wagon that would take him home.

And now I want to turn and walk away,
run away, back to the train
and make it take us home to Akwesasne
and hope my father will be there at the station
to take Mattie and me home.

But it is just a dream, a hopeless dream,
where Mattie and I would be home
with our whole family there,
all our brothers and our sisters
and our father
and our mother.

Mother

AKE'NISTENHA

mattie

"You children," a man calls out.

Sarah and I stand on the platform,
alone in a river of people who rush
hurriedly to and from the train.

"You children for da school?"

He moves toward us, this man,
who looks older than Father,
this man with hair thick and gray
that curls down around his ears.

But instead of the sad look
my father now wears every day,
this man's mouth spreads wide
across his face into a smile.

Sarah and I nod,
but we do not move.

"C'mon now," he says.

My feet remain fixed firmly
in place on the platform
as I watch this man closely.

I search my mind for some memory
of other men who look like him.
I recall no one, no one whose skin

is as black as the coal
that burns in our kitchen stove.

"C'mon. I ain't got all day," he says quickly,
though not unkindly. "Where yo' things be?"

I nod to the wooden box that sits
on the platform beside us,
one that holds so little because
when we packed for our trip
Father said we would need so little.
He said all would be provided for us,
even our clothes, which makes no sense
because we have our own clothes.

But that's what he was told
by the lady and man who came
and sat at our kitchen table
one summer night.

I wish this man as black as coal
were not here to take us to the school.

I wish it were our father
who was finding us at the station,
telling us it is time to go,
time to go home.

RAKE'NIHA

Father

"Take care of your sister," Father said to me
as Sarah and I boarded the train

for our long journey away from home.

"HE'EN," I answered.

Yes. I will take care of my sister.

"Speak English now," he commanded.
"They will expect it."

I nodded.

"Promise me."

"HE'EN. Yes, Father, I will," I assured him.

Poor Father.

He knows deep in his heart
that Sarah and I did not want
to leave our home.

Father said it would be best,
best for us, best for our family,
and that we had to be good.

"Be good," he said to us,
though his eyes looked only at me.

"Yes, Father," I answered him. HE'EN.
It's hard to think in English.

Sarah is better than I am
at being good,
but she stands next to me

and does not move.
She stares at this man
who is the blackest man
we have ever seen.

"Come, Sarah," I say loudly.

I do not want this man
to think I am afraid.

I won't be afraid.
I won't.

I hope I can be good.

saraн

"C'mon, now," he says as he sets our box
up on the strangest, strangest thing on wheels
I have ever seen, where several pairs of eyes
stare down at us.

So many, many strange things.

"Climb up," he urges, his voice friendly
but so strong that I dare not disobey.

Yet my legs will not move,
and my feet cling fast to the ground.

Even Mattie holds back;
Mattie, who is older and braver than I am,
Mattie, who is not afraid of anything,
stands and stares at this strange contraption,
this wooden wagon with no sides,
this strange wagon with iron wheels
that rest on railroad tracks just like the train
that brought us here.

"C'mon now," he says again,
beckoning to us with his whole hand,
"dis ol' herdig won't bite;
da herdig gonna take you home."

Home?

Akwesasne?

I turn to look at the train behind us.
People hurrying about, climbing aboard.
The train could take us home.

And as I turn my head back toward
this strange machine on wheels,
Mattie is being lifted up by two thick black arms.

"C'mon, missy, Davis ain't got all day," he says, turning toward me.

But before those big black arms swing back for me,
I scramble up the wooden boxes placed on the ground
as steps beside this strange train wagon
and plop quickly down next to Mattie.

The black man laughs loudly, and in one step
he, too, is on the wagon, his hands grabbing hold of a wooden handle.

Suddenly this strange cart jerks, and Mattie and I cling to each other
as it starts rolling forward along the tracks.

"Welcome to Carlisle," the man's voice booms behind us.
"You children gonna be awright now. You children gonna like dis place.
Dis place gonna be yo' new home."

Home?

Mattie

The wheels of the cart roll noisily
along the tracks,
squeaking and squealing.

There has been noise everywhere
since we left home, strange noise.

Especially people noise,
people whose voices are loud and harsh
even when they are not angry.

Even when my father was stern,
even when my mother would scold,
their voices were not loud and harsh.

Sometimes my mother said
we were making too much noise
when we ran through the house
when we were children playing.

Sarah and I make no noise now
as we sit next to each other
on our way to the school.

sarah

"Mattie," I whisper to my sister as we stand
side by side on the grass.

"What?" she answers quickly,
but not impatiently.

"Stay with me," I demand.

She grips my hand so tightly that,
if we had been at home, I would have thought
she was being bossy like she can be sometimes
because she thinks she is grown up.

Mattie is my older sister
and sometimes she can be mean.
I think it is because she is smaller than I am
and that should not be if I am her little sister.

She says she does not care, but I think she does.

She says she is not small. She says I am big.
But that is not true because
Hazel Lazore and I are the same age
and I am no taller than Hazel,
and Mattie is smaller than Hazel's sister Emma
and Emma and Mattie were born the same year.

My sister now holds my hand tightly,
but she is not being mean.

Fifteen, maybe twenty of us,
I did not dare lean forward long enough to count,
stand in a long line outside in the sunshine,
in front of the big white building,
white as the newest snow in October on the outside
but dark and damp inside despite the many windows,
this big, white building where Mattie and I will now sleep.

And some of these children who stand beside us
are as scary as Mr. Davis, who is the blackest man
I have ever seen in my twelve years
of being a human being,
Mr. Davis, who found us at the train station
and brought us to the school with four other children who
sat and stared at Mattie and me. And said nothing.
Nor we to them.

And now these children and Mattie and I
and others who appeared from nowhere
stand in a line, a strange assortment of dress
and hair and sizes. Yet all of us as brown
as the soil in my father's garden
when it has been warmed by the sun.

I hold Mattie's hand tightly as, looking to my right,
I see an enormous figure full of blackness
moving stiffly down the line,
stopping and staring at each child.
At some she scowls and nods and passes by,
but at others she stops and tilts her head and stares,
and then thick white fingers reach through
the end of a long black sleeve, gripping a shoulder,
pulling a child forward.

Without a word, she moves the child to left or right,
and then steps back and glances up and down the line
and nods and then moves on,
coming closer to where Mattie and I stand,
holding our breath and hands tightly.

I do not want to be moved.

Please, please, please.
Do not take me from my sister.

When the blackness stops in front of Mattie,
I hear my sister suck in her breath and let it out
through her teeth, but I hold my breath in altogether
and look down at the dust on my shoes.

As I feel Mattie's body being pulled forward,
she grips my right hand even more tightly
and my arm lifts upward to move with her.

Smack!

A sharpness hits me unexpectedly
on the edge of my wrist,
and Mattie and I are instantly apart
and the breath I was holding inside explodes.

I look up in time to see thick white fingers
moving toward Mattie's shoulder,
and before I can utter a word of protest,
Mattie is snatched forward,
and as my eyes fix on the beady black eyes,
they turn sharply to return my stare,
forcing mine downward once more.

And suddenly Mattie's shoes appear
on the other side of me,
and I feel the fingers of her right hand
pressing strongly into the palm of my left.

"Will that do?" the blur of blackness calls out
from the end of the row.

"Yes, Mrs. Dwyer," a man in a tall black hat answers
as he looks into a box sitting on wooden legs.
"It will do."

"Now, children," he adds in a loud voice.
"Let's smile."

I wonder if anyone smiled.

MATTIE

We stand on the grass
in front of the large white building
where we left our belongings,
our only ties with home
except each other.

Across the yard,
a man in a tall black hat
stands by himself peering into a box
which sits on tall wooden legs.
We had watched him, silently,
as he spread the wooden legs apart
and placed his box high on top.

"Mattie," Sarah whispers.

"What?" I ask.

I hear the fear in her voice.

I know she is frightened.

We stand in a long line
with other children,
children we do not know,
children who do not speak
our language,
nor we theirs,
and if any speak as much
English as Sarah and I do,

we would not know because
no one has spoken to us.

"Stay with me," she says,
looking past me.
Her voice shakes slightly,
and her hand grips mine so tightly
that I glance to my right to determine
the cause of her concern.

A woman taller than Edna Cook,
who is the woman who lives next door
to my grandmother's house, appears.
This woman, who wears a dress so black
that she could disappear into the night
when there is no moon,
pulls a child forward from the line.

And before I can think to wonder
where this child is going,
she is pushed firmly
back into the row,
three girls away
from her former line mate.

The mass of black rustles closer.

Sarah squeezes my hand
as this woman
taller than Edna Cook
stops in front of me.

I draw in a deep breath
and stare into two eyes that look

like tiny chunks of coal
set into a snowbank
muddied by a January thaw.

When she returns my stare,
a cold shiver spreads up my back,
and I momentarily forget
it is an early afternoon
in late summer.

As I lower my stare,
my errant eyes focus briefly
on a silver pin,
or perhaps it is a watch,
fastened to her dress.

Suddenly, soundlessly,
my body surges forward,
my left hand still clinging tightly
to Sarah's right.

And then the quiet is broken
as the smack of wood on flesh
rings sharply in my ears
just seconds before I feel
the stinging of my skin;
and just seconds before my eyes
begin to well with tears,
I am already standing
next to my sister once more.

The fingers of my right hand
reach out to assure her
we are still together;

I press my fingers firmly
into the palm of her hand,
silently urging her to say nothing,
pushing my left wrist hard against
the back of my leg to dull the pain.

Through my blurry vision
I see the man in the black hat.
He waves and calls out to us,
but I do not hear what he says
because the noise of shame
still rings in my ears
and his words evaporate into the air.

sarah

I open my eyes and let them adjust to the darkness
of the early morning,
and wonder if I should rise and dress.

I am always awake before the dawn.

I prop myself up on my elbows
and look across the beds of strangers
to where Mattie lies sleeping.

I have never had to sleep with strangers.

When we readied for bed last night,
there was a chilling silence throughout the room
as the woman in the black dress
and a younger woman dressed in brown
pointed out the nightgown placed on each bed
and then stood in the center of the room
until all of us readied for bed, all of us strangers,
readying for bed together in silence.

And then the woman in the black dress
told us to kneel for our bedtime prayers,
and many of the other children stood still,
silently staring at the floor,
until she pointed at those of us who knew,
who understood, who did what it was she wanted.

But while she shouted out some words whose
meanings meant nothing to me,
I asked the Creator to help me to be good

so that we could someday go home,
but then I thought about home
and so I added that I was thankful
for all that Mother Earth has given to us
and thankful that our father is doing
what is best for us.

And when I was done, I waited and waited and waited
for the woman in the black dress to finish,
and when she was, Mattie and I,
and some of the other children,
rose instantly to our feet,
and soon the others followed.

And now I am awake while
all those strangers are still sound asleep.

And so is Mattie.

But Mattie is in her own bed now.

When the two women turned out the lights
last night and closed the door behind them,
only seconds of silence filled the room before
I heard the muffled sounds of tears echoing my own,
and only seconds more went by before I heard
the creaking of springs and sensed Mattie
standing beside me.

"Shh," she whispered as she lifted the blanket
and slid into my bed and laid her left arm
gently across my waist.

"We won't cry," she scolded softly in my ear.

I pressed my face into the pillow
and silenced my sobs,
and with my sister's forehead pressed
against my back, I fell asleep listening
to the muffled sounds of tears
echoing those in my heart.

And now Mattie is in her own bed, sleeping,
and I wonder if I should rise and dress.

MATTIE

"Mattie."

I hear a voice, far away,
in the distant corners of my head.

It is Sarah whispering softly,
and, for just a moment,
I think we are at home.

But as I peer through
my partially opened eyes,
I see Sarah standing beside me,
wearing a drab brown dress
that makes my younger sister
look old and dreary.

Where is her blue dress
that she hung on the peg
when we went to bed?

For just a moment,
I think I am dreaming.

"Mattie, Mattie, get up," Sarah says.

She tugs at my shoulder,
pulling the coarse, gray blanket back,
letting the morning chill creep in.

It is no dream.

As I lift myself up slowly
to stretch out the stiffness of sleep,
my brain bolts at the sound of a voice
sharply barking commands.

"What's this? What's this? Not ready?"

Before I am even out of my bed,
before my eyes have adjusted
to the dimness of the morning light,
Sarah hands me a pile of clothes,
a pile of dark, drab dreariness
that matches what I see her wearing,
and with an almost tearful "hurry"
she vanishes from my side.

"Come, come, girls, line up."

I frantically pull on the long black stockings
as a blur of blackness appears beside me,
but I am hurrying too much to look up,
and, besides, I do not need to look to know
it is the woman in the black dress.

"Matilda Tarbell!"

She knows my name.
She knows who I am.

I do not remember her name,
but I know who she is.

"The first step to becoming a productive person,
Matilda, is learning to follow rules,

and rising and being ready to start the day
with everyone else is the first rule here."

I am hurrying to start the day,
but it is already too late.

Perhaps I can pretend,
pretend I do not understand her.
So many children here do not.

Speak English now. They will expect it.

"Do you understand?" she demands,
rapping her stick against the palm of her hand.

I do not want to feel the shame of her stick.

"Yes, ma'am. I understand."

I will try to be good, Father.

I will.

saraн

"Hold still," a girl bigger and older than I am says
as she brushes my hair hard against my head,
the bristles scraping sharply against my skin.

I can brush my own hair,
my hair that is longer and darker than even Mattie's,
my hair that is almost as long as my mother's was,
my hair that flows down my back and stays away
from my face with the two combs that my mother
bought me for my birthday when I was ten.

Sometimes when I was angry at Mattie because
she was so bossy, my mother would nod and smile
and slide the combs away and run her fingers through my hair
and tell me how she was making peace for me and Mattie,
how when the KAIANEREKOWA, the Great Law of Peace, was created,
Hiawatha and the Peacemaker had to comb out the snakes
from the hair of the TADODAHO, the great chief.

We would sit together on the wooden steps of our porch,
and as her fingers fell through my hair,
so would my anger fall away,
and I would be at peace with my sister once more.

But here in this room full of strangers,
I feel no peace.

My hair is being pulled and pinned
and twisted and turned and knotted
until I feel a lump of hand and hair being
pressed into the back of my neck.

"You will have to learn to do this for yourself,"
the voice behind me commands.

I say nothing.

"Maybe she should have it cut, Ida,"
another voice adds, causing me to leap
forward from the wooden stool so quickly
that I almost fall to the floor.

"Now look what you've done," says an angry voice
that must be Ida. "I'll have to start again," she adds
as she pulls me by the hair back up onto the stool.

A dozen eyes stare at me from the bench along the wall,
eyes that belong to girls who watch and wait,
one girl holding on to the ends of her long, black braids
with fists clenched tightly against her chest,
another leaning so far forward she surely will fall,
the others shrinking back into the wooden wall behind them.

A dozen eyes stare at me
but none of them belong to Mattie.

AKTSI:'A

my older sister

Where is my older sister?

Mattie

I lift my spoon and let the broth
drip back into the bowl.
There is nothing in the bowl
except brown liquid.

The girl across from me
smiles and lifts her spoon.

"Soup," she whispers.

I know it is soup.

"I know," I say.

I stir my spoon slowly
and stare into the metal bowl
wondering where the rest
of the soup might be.

"You speak English," she says.

She sounds surprised.

"Yes," I answer.

"So many don't, you know,"
she says, lowering her voice
as though she has revealed
some great secret to me.

Sarah and I can speak English.

If we try.

If we want to.

"It's not very good, is it?" she says.

At first I think she means my English.

Then I see she is nodding her head
downward toward the bowl,
and I know she means the soup.

I shake my head.

"No," I agree. "It isn't.
There's nothing in it."

She nods.

"My grandmother makes
the best soup you have ever tasted,"
she says quietly, looking around
as though she wants no one else to hear.
"It takes a long time to make
and it has corn and beans—"

"Mine did, too," I interrupt.

Our eyes meet.

"I'm Gracie," she says.

Perhaps I have a friend.

saraн

"Ruthie," our teacher says. "Stand up."

"Stand up, Ruthie," she says again, louder.

No one moves.

I try to look around the room,
without looking around the room,
to see who should be standing up.

I cannot remember who was named Ruthie.

No one in the room stands up.
No one moves.

Soon our teacher steps toward a small girl
whose face is buried in her arms,
which are folded on the wooden desk,
two rows away from me.

She does not see the teacher coming,
and so I hold my breath for her.

But the teacher does not have a stick in her hand,
like the woman in the black dress,
and when she is beside the girl's desk,
she does not strike her.

Instead, she touches her lightly on the shoulder,
and her voice is soft when she speaks,
not sharp like the woman in the black dress.

"Ruthie," she says, tapping her finger
on top of the girl's shoulder several times.
"Ruthie," she says again. "Stand up."

The girl lifts her head so slowly,
showing no surprise, showing no fear;
so I think she must have heard the teacher's voice,
must have heard her movement,
must have known she was there.

But when this girl looks up from where she sits,
her dark eyes, browner than even my own,
stare into the eyes of the teacher,
and the skin of her forehead
crinkles questioningly toward her.

"Ruth-ie," the teacher repeats firmly,
her finger tapping—one—two—three times
where a paper is pinned to Ruthie's dress.

"Stand up, please, Ruth-ie."

And now she takes her elbow and gently
lifts her to her feet, so that she is standing
beside the wooden desk, but as Ruthie rises,
her head drops and her eyes drift downward
until her chin rests almost on her chest.

Our teacher puts her hand under Ruthie's chin
and lifts her head until their eyes meet again.

"Ruth-ie," she says once more, and nods her head.

The teacher wants her to say her name,
her new name, her school name.

But Ruthie says nothing.

Mattie and I did not need new names.
Our teacher liked our names.
She said they were good names,
that our parents gave us good names.

She does not even know,
and we will not tell her,
that we have other names,
other names which are special names.

When Father told us we were going away,
going far away from home to school,
he said we should only tell our English names.

He said our Mohawk names are special,
and we should keep them for special times.

MATTIE

My father said,
"You will go to school."

He said,
"They will teach you
what you must learn."

I said I could learn just as well
if I stayed home.

He could teach me.

My father said,
"You must go to school.
Life will be better for you.
It is for the best."

So we came to school
because he said it would be best,
best for me and best for Sarah,
best for our brothers and sisters
who went to other schools,
some closer to home,
some farther away,
than Sarah and I are now.

But the first thing we learned
was how to march.

If I wanted to march,
I would have joined the army

and become a soldier
like Uncle Lewis,
my father's brother
who is as young
as my oldest brother,
except maybe,
just maybe,
Father would have been
even more sad.

When Uncle Lewis told us
he had decided to join
President Taft's army,
Father shook his head
and his eyes filled with sadness.

As we stood in the front yard
and watched Uncle Lewis leave,
catching a ride with the milk wagon
heading to town and the train station
and to President Taft's army,
wherever that was,
Father shook his head
and shook his head
and his eyes filled with sadness.

When the milk wagon
melted into the sun,
Father turned and walked
through the field of uncut hay
to the edge of the river
and stood there
for hours and hours

and hours.

I wonder.

I wonder if Father
walked through the field
behind our house
to the edge of the river
and stood there

for hours and hours

and hours

when Sarah
and I left for this school.

I wonder if Father knew
that when we came to school
we would learn how to march
like Uncle Lewis.

I wonder if our brothers and sisters
who went to other schools
learned how to march.

When we rise at dawn,
we march to our morning meal.
When that meal is done,
we march to our lessons.
When we finish our lessons,
we march to our midday meal.
When that meal is done,
we march to our work.

And on
and on
we march
throughout the day.

Today, Miss Prentiss,
who shows us how to use a machine
that sews our clothes,
made us march around the room.

We marched and marched.

To stretch our legs, she said,
so we could pump the pedal
that turns the wheel which moves
the needle up and down.

If I thought marching all day
would stretch my legs
and make me tall,
I would march

and march

and march.

But marching
only makes me tired.

sarah

Sitting at my desk, I feel its woodenness
against my elbows and the backs of my knees.
My legs ache to run through the fields,
searching for strawberries, even though
the berries have long been gone from the fields
at home, replaced by the black-eyed Susans
found scattered behind our home,
black-eyed Susans that my arms long to pick.

"Sarah," I hear a voice call, and for merely a moment
I think it is my mother calling me from the fields.

But it is not my mother.

It is Miss Weston who wants my attention.

"Sarah," she calls again. "It is your turn to read."

I slowly rise to my feet, dreading the task.

I like to read, and I am becoming a better reader,
but it is hard to read English
and I do not want to stand beside my desk
and read out loud while other students stare
even though I know they stare because
they do not know what I read.

I open the book and begin.
But it is hard to read when you are
looking at words in English and thinking
of strawberries in the fields at home.

"Speak up, Sarah," Miss Weston insists.

My heart jumps into my mouth and so I stop reading
as my eyes search frantically over the words
which have become a blur of blackness.

"I have lost my place," I whisper,
closing my eyes quickly, hoping the words
will have become untangled when I look again.

But when I open my eyes, I see Miss Weston's hand
draped over the top of my book, pointing to
a place on the page where I must begin.

"Start here," she says, firmly, but not unkindly.

I wish I could like Miss Weston,
but I do not think Miss Weston likes me.

Mattie says I should be good for Miss Weston,
which should make me laugh because Miss Weston
is the only person Mattie is good for.

MATTIE

Miss Weston.
She is the nicest teacher
in the whole school.

She returned the piece I had written
about the baskets my mother made,
and at the top of the paper,
in beautiful handwriting, she had written:

How beautifully you write!

"Sarah," I say,
"Miss Weston is the only teacher,
the only teacher in the whole school."

She looks up at me,
her big brown eyes opened wide
in her very typical Sarah
"what are you talking about?" look.

"We have lots of teachers," she says.

I sigh. It is so Sarah.

"Too many teachers," she adds,
shaking her head from side to side.

Sarah likes to learn,
but she does not like our teachers.
She says they scold and scowl
and make us stand to speak or read

but never to share our thoughts.

I like to know,
but I do not always like to learn
what others think I should,
and, like Sarah,
I do not like the teachers either,
except Miss Weston,
who does not scold or scowl.

Except Miss Weston,
who looks at us when she asks us
to stand and speak or read.

Except Miss Weston,
who says I write beautifully.

"But look," I say.

I hold out my paper
so she can share my pride
as we sit side by side on her bed.

"So?" she replies sharply.

With a shrug of her shoulders,
she rises quickly from the bed
and stands by the window,
pretending that something
outside draws her deep attention.

I glance down to see the edge of a paper
peeking out from under her book.
I slide it out carefully, quietly.

You can do better. . . .

I still think Miss Weston
is the best teacher,
the very best teacher
in the whole school.

Sarah is just jealous.

saraн

Swish . . . Swish . . . Swish

The sweep of the broom against
the rough stone steps brushes against my ears.

I peer through the partly opened window,
stained and streaked with the dirt of years,
and watch as Mr. Davis pulls the broom
back and forth across the steps in strong strokes.

Swish . . . Swish . . . Swish

"No one calls me *Mister* Davis," he told me yesterday
when I thanked him for fixing the handle on my bureau.
"I's just Davis. Dere ain't never been a *Mister* Davis
in my family. Not ever."

And then he laughed quietly and shook his head
from side to side, and I wondered what I had said,
what I could have said that amused him so.

"Davis!"

The sharpness of the voice caught me by surprise,
but I did not need to turn my head to know
that Mrs. Dwyer had entered the room.

She stood just inside the doorway
and peered over the tops of the tiny glasses
she sometimes wears, closely examining
the space where the door meets the wall.

"It looks to me like your job in here
is finished," she said coldly.

"Yessum," Mr. Davis answered quickly.

The laughter had left his voice,
and when he left the room, his head hung so low
that his chin almost rested on his chest,
and when he passed by Mrs. Dwyer,
she rapped her ruler—*tap, tap, tap*—
against the palm of her hand
and scowled at him,
and after he had left,
she turned her head toward me
and scowled at me.

"Girls! Line up for dinner," she demanded,
rapping her ruler—*tap, tap, tap*—
against the palm of her hand.

Thank you, Mr. Davis, I mouth soundlessly
as I watch him sweeping the dirt off the steps.

Swish . . . Swish . . . Swish

Thank you for being my friend.

MATTIE

Miss Weston said my essay was so good
it should be printed in *The Arrow*.
She said she would show my essay
to the "man on the bandstand,"
and then she whispered to me
that the "man on the bandstand"
—who puts our paper in print—
was not a man at all,
but a very nice woman,
and someone who would like my essay.

Then Mrs. Dwyer found out her plan.
She was very, very angry,
angrier than I have ever seen her,
and I have seen Mrs. Dwyer very angry.

In her very stiff voice, Mrs. Dwyer said,
"We need essays on moral instruction
more than we need essays on baskets."

When Mrs. Dwyer said she would tell
the "man on the bandstand"
that my essay,
my beautiful essay
about my mother's baskets,
was not to be printed,
my heart fell into my feet,
and if I had not told Sarah
that we were not to cry,
I would have shed a thousand tears.

I didn't tell Sarah.

I told Gracie, Gracie Powless,
whose bed is next to mine because
Sarah could not have that bed,
Mrs. Dwyer would not let her,
and now Gracie is my friend,
maybe my best friend.

The night before the morning
that I gave my essay to Miss Weston,
I read it out loud to Gracie,
because Gracie doesn't read very well.

When she heard what I had written,
she leaned forward on her bed
and sighed and said she wished
she could write like I do.
She said my writing was good,
so good that if she closed her eyes,
and listened to my words,
she could almost see the baskets,
the beautiful baskets
that my mother made.

So when I told Gracie
that Mrs. Dwyer was angry,
and would not let Miss Weston
put my essay in the school paper,
she said she felt like crying.
That is when I knew that
what Mrs. Dwyer said didn't matter,
didn't matter at all,

because Gracie,
whose bed is next to mine,
had become my friend,
my best friend.

saraн

"I want to go home," I tell Mattie
as we sit at the table in the study room,
where she is helping me with my essay.

"Well, we can't," she says in her scolding voice.

"I will never write as well as you do," I tell her.
"Besides, Miss Weston yells at me."

When I see the look in Mattie's eyes,
I know I should not have said that.
She likes Miss Weston.

"Miss Weston doesn't yell at anyone," she snaps.
"If you would write about something that made sense,
you would find it easier."

Mattie does not like my essay.

Neither did Miss Weston.

I wrote about living in the sky
and how the sun and the moon
were my father and mother
and the stars were my sisters and brothers.
The sky was an endless sea of blue
like the river that flows behind our house.
My father was the setting sun
and my mother a harvest moon
and so they looked more alike than different
and they could always be seen at the same time.

We star children would sit on the clouds
and listen to our mother tell stories
and watch our father fish in the sky river.

Mattie said I had it all wrong,
that if I was going to write about the sky
then the moon should be our Grandmother
and the Sun our eldest Brother.

I tried to tell her it was my story
and that I could tell it any way I wanted to,
but she just kept saying it made no sense.

Miss Weston just said it had no ending,
and that I could do better.

I liked it even if it had no ending,
even if I had many words spelled wrong.

"It is too hard," I tell my sister,
who writes better than I do,
who spells better than I do.

"It's not too hard," she says, "if you try."

I think I try all the time.

I will never be as good in school as Mattie.

I stare at the paper, smudged where Mattie
has corrected some of my spelling,
and I think that Miss Weston is right.
It is not a very good story. It is not real,
and, besides, I do not want to live in the sky.

I want to go home
and live with my mother and father
and all my sisters and brothers
in our home by the river.

But they are not there,
not my brothers and sisters
who are scattered in schools
in places far far away from home,
not my brothers and sisters
who came and left our mother and father
and lie buried in the ground by the river.

"Do you like it here?" I ask Mattie
as she slides my paper back to me.

"It doesn't matter what we like," she says.

I pretend I am writing on my paper so that
Mattie will not see the tears I am trying to keep
inside my eyes because if she sees me cry
she will be angry again.

MATTIE

I told Sarah
if she cried again,
one more time,
over anything,
I would smack her.

And I would.

She thinks she is
the only one
who is homesick,

the only one
who misses family,

the only one
who longs for
our father and mother
and sisters and brothers
and childhood friends.

She is too big to cry.

Childhood is over.

saraн

I will not cry.

I will not cry.

I will not cry.

MATTIE

"Hurry," Gracie says.

"You will be late again," she adds
just before she disappears
into the hall.

"I'm trying," I tell her empty space
as I tie my shoes as quickly as my fingers
will work with the laces.

I can't be late again.

Not again.

It's hard to wake up in the morning when,
in the early hours before dawn,
I have just begun to sleep.

It's even hard to wake up when
the morning bell ringing over and over
sounds like a distant echo in my head.

It's even hard to wake up when Sarah,
poking my side with her finger,
warns me I will be in trouble.
Again.

So by the time my eyes
are willing to wake
and my body agrees
to ease out of my bed,

I cannot wash and dress
fast enough not to be late.

I hope it is Miss Prentiss,
and not Mrs. Dwyer,
who watches as we march off
to our morning meal.

Miss Prentiss tries to scowl
like Mrs. Dwyer,
especially if dour Mrs. Dwyer
is in the room,
but if I am late
she will turn her head
and pretend she does not see me
as I slip into the line behind Gracie.

My shoes tied, I spring from my bed
and flee out the door into the hall
just as the girls at the front of the line
begin marching out the door
past Miss Prentiss.

Safe.

saraн

The days go by so slowly,
and they are always the same,
an emptiness full of work and lessons
and a longing for home.

Mattie says I should make friends,
that I would not miss home so much if I had a friend.

She is wrong.

I would miss our home even if I had a friend.

Mattie has Gracie
and so now she likes being here.

I hope she has not forgotten our home.

I wonder if I will ever see my home again.

One of the older girls, Ida, who bragged that
when she first came here to the Carlisle Indian School,
her ride on the train was the longest one anyone
had ever taken, that she had traveled through
mountains so tall they pierced the sky
and land so flat that the sun seemed to stay forever,
said she has never been home.

Ida says this is her home now.

She says she has been here at school since
she was ten years old, and now she is older than Mattie

and very tall and scowls so much I think
she has been here as long as Mrs. Dwyer.

Most of the bigger girls have rooms on the first floor
and I wonder why Ida does not have her bed there.

I wonder if the older, bigger girls are her friends.

I wonder if you can live at a school as long as Ida has
and have no friends.

I will try to make friends,
but I do not think Ida will be one of them.

I will try to be good
so Father will be proud of me.

I will try not to cry
so Mattie will not be angry with me.

But this will never be my home.

Mattie

For the first time
I notice the words
written high on the wall
above the chalkboard.

LABOR CONQUERS ALL THINGS

Perhaps it is because Miss Weston
has just taught us a new word—*conquer.*

She wrote it in large letters
on the chalkboard
and then used her pointing stick
to show us it was the same word
as the one on the wall.

And then she said,
"Labor conquers all things,"
and the sound of Mrs. Dwyer's voice
saying those same words
soon after we arrived
rang in my head.

She had stood in the doorway
of the room where we sleep
after we had dressed for the day.
We stood in a line
at the foot of our beds
as she, one by one,
stood before us
and told us where

we would report
for our work.

Now Miss Weston
stands in the front of the room
and says the same words,
and I push the image
quickly from my head
because I cannot bear to put
Miss Weston and Mrs. Dwyer
in the same thought.

saraн

"Come look," I call to Ruthie,
who sits on the edge of her bed,
pretending to read.

Her bed is next to mine,
and I would like to be her friend
but I do not think she wants to be mine
because she never tries to talk to me.

Mattie says she is just shy
and that if I want her for my friend,
I will have to do all the work.

"Ruthie, look," I say again,
beckoning with my finger.

She likes to be called
Pretty Feather when we are alone
because it is her real name in English,
but I do not want to be in trouble,
so I call her by her new name
and still hope she will want to be my friend.

"What?" she asks as she leaves the book behind
and steps to the window to stand beside me.

"Look," I say as I nod toward the ground below.

A rabbit sits motionless on the grassy area
beneath the window, its ears straight up,
listening for danger.

"A rabbit," I say, pointing.

"A rabbit," she repeats, and then says
a word I do not understand.

"I wonder if there are others," I add,
searching left and right, even though
I know she does not understand me.

She imitates me, looking from left to right,
shrugs her shoulders and returns to her bed
and opens her book, which I know she cannot read.

"Where I come from, we have a dance we call
the rabbit dance," I tell her, even though
I know she does not understand all the words I say.
"I could tell you about it."

She looks up, yet as soon as our eyes meet,
her attention returns to her book,
but I know she is pretending,
only pretending to read,
because she does not ever turn a page.

I do not read English as well as Mattie,
but I know enough to turn the pages.

"Would you like to hear about it?"

Her eyes stare at the book lying in her lap,
but she does not answer, and though I know
she does not understand all my words,
I wish she did because
I would like her to be my friend.

MATTIE

"How silly," I say to Gracie,
who wants us to spend our free time
watching the boys at practice
running around a field,
throwing and kicking a ball.

"Who wants to watch boys throw
themselves into each other?" I ask.

"I do," she answers softly,
looking at the floor so I will not see
the smile on her face.

"You don't like this game,"
I say sharply, knowing it is Thomas,
who fits his real name, Flying Deer,
not the game, that she likes to watch.

"Yes, I do," she answers again.

"Running around on the grass,
trying to catch a ball,
and getting thrown to the ground
even when you don't have a chance of
catching the ball, is silly," I add.

"Now, if it were a game like,
hmm, let's say lacrosse,
that requires some skill,
it would most certainly not be

a waste of our time," I say lightly,
as though my choice of sport
was so very important.

She lifts her chin to assert herself,
and when I see the smile has vanished
from her face, I am sorry that I teased her,
the best friend I have ever had.

"All right," I say, jumping up
from the edge of my bed,
where I had been reading.

"I still think it is silly—
very, very silly—
but let's go watch this silly game,"
I add, laughing lightly,
pretending I do not see the hurt,
so she knows I am not laughing at her.

Her smile returns
and she, too, laughs,
and I know I have been forgiven.

"You are right." She nods. "It is silly.
But it is still fun to watch."

Arm in arm, side by side,
we head toward the door,
friends, sisters at heart,
off to share our free time
watching the young man
who has caught Gracie's heart.

But as we stride
arm in arm down the hall,
a sharp voice stops us short.

"Girls! Where are you going?"

The muscles of Gracie's arm tighten.

I do not need to turn my head to know
whose voice echoes in my ears,
and I know Gracie also knows,
but neither Gracie nor I speak.

"Answer me," Mrs. Dwyer demands.
"Where are you going?"

I know Gracie will not answer.
Gracie never answers Mrs. Dwyer,
who thinks Gracie does not speak
English as well as she does,
who does not know my friend
is often quiet out of fear.

"Just out," I answer. "For a walk."

I try to make my voice sound soft,
and as I turn to face her sour face,
I try to keep my eyes cast down,
but they are stubborn
and will not obey me,
and when my eyes meet hers,
I know the softness of my voice
cannot cover the anger in my eyes.

"It is not free time, yet,"
she responds sharply.
"Are your lessons finished?"

"Yes, they are," I tell her.

I answer for us both,
for even though I know
that mine are done,
I know that Gracie
finds her studies hard
and often leaves her lessons long
before they're finished.

Gracie's eyes now search the floor,
and I know she will not answer.

So I must answer for us both.

"Gracie, look at me," she commands,
waving her ruler in the air
in front of Gracie's face.

"Look—at—me," Mrs. Dwyer says again
slowly and very, very loudly,
as though Gracie cannot hear,
thinking Gracie cannot understand.

If my heart were not beating so hard,
if I did not know there was no laughter,
no kindness, in this woman's heart,
if I did not know Gracie's heart
was trembling in fear,

I would laugh to think that she thinks
Gracie cannot hear or understand.

Gracie looks up,
but she does not answer.

"Are—your—lessons—finished?"
Mrs. Dwyer asks again. "Are they?"

I let my arm slide down Gracie's,
cupping her hand in mine,
squeezing lightly in assurance,
hoping that her lessons are done,
hoping she will say yes,
hoping she will be strong enough
to stand her ground.

But Gracie says nothing.

Instead, her head moves slowly
from side to side in response
while Mrs. Dwyer bobs her head
up and down confidently,
knowingly, accusingly.

She raps her ruler lightly,
but rapidly, into the palm
of her left hand as she speaks,
looking not at Gracie but at me.

"I expect you to be industrious,
and I expect you to be honest.
If you are not industrious,
you will accomplish nothing.

If you are not honest in everything,
you will be trusted about nothing."

She is not looking at Gracie
when she says this.

She is looking at me.

Our eyes meet
but there is nothing I can say.

"Return to your studies," she adds,
pointing her ruler toward the door.

Gracie turns and pulls me
back into the room,
where dreams are allowed
only in our sleep,
where even the thought
of a handsome young man
is not powerful enough
to make Gracie strong.

I want to say something,
but I dare not say a word.

There is nothing I can say.

saraн

"Your sister better be careful," Ida hisses at me
as she stares icily across the table
as we sit in the dining hall at our morning meal.

I stare into the bowl of oatmeal that had lost its warmth
before I even took my first mouthful.

I do not think Ida likes me,
but I do not know why.

"When Mrs. Dwyer makes me captain," she continues,
"your sister better cooperate more and have a better attitude,
or she will be in serious trouble."

I want to ask her what it means to be captain.
I want to ask her what it means to cooperate.

But I say nothing.

"Are you listening to me?" she snaps.

Ida is even bossier than Mattie.

MATTIE

"Very nice, Mattie," says Miss Prentiss.

She fingers the fabric
where I have carefully
mended a tear in someone's apron.

The mending is endless,
and I often wonder
whose dress,
whose shirt,
whose cape it is
I make whole again.

But I never know.

The mending is endless,
and I often wonder:
How did this tear,
this rip,
this slit occur?

But I never know.

I did not need Miss Prentiss
to teach me how to sew and mend.

My mother did that.

When my mother and I mended,
we knew what had caused the tear:
that the sleeve had fought with a nail,

the hem had been trapped by a shoe,
the trousers had battled with the stones.

We knew.

"You do very nice work," she adds,
taking the lifeless garment from me.
"I will have someone else iron this."

She surprises me.

We mend. We iron. We fold.
This is school. The routine is clear.
We mend. We iron. We fold.

Sometimes I use a machine,
my right foot pumping up and down
to make the needle move in and out
through the material.

But sometimes I let my hands
do the stitching
instead of the machine,
the way I mended and sewed at home.
Then I do not mind the work as much.

Miss Prentiss stands quietly beside me,
studying the mending intently,
the mending I did with my hands.

"I think I will let you do the finer work,"
she continues, surprising me once more.

Then she lifts my right hand,

running her thumb
back and forth lightly
over the tops of my fingers.

A blurry image of my mother
holding my hands
begins to surface,
and her soft voice whispers
somewhere in my memory.

Your tiny hands, Mattie. They are a gift.

I close my eyes,
and I am home,
sitting beside my mother
as we work together,
sewing and mending.

AKE'NISTENHA

Mother

"Yes, yes. That is what we will do."

An empty voice, a loveless voice,
brings me back to the present
and when I see it is Miss Prentiss,
stiff Miss Prentiss,
who stands beside me,
inspecting my fingers as though
they are no part of my being,
I draw my hand back slowly,
carefully, cautiously,
from her unwelcome touch.

saraн

I wish I were Mattie.

When Mattie is not at lessons, she works
where the autumn wind coming in an open window
might cool the room where she sits at a machine
and sews or mends the clothes we wear.

I wish I did not work in the laundry,
where it smells so strong of soap
and is so hot that no open window
can make a difference.

I wish I did not work in the laundry,
even if Miss Velma, kind Miss Velma,
who is the nicest person at the school,
except for maybe Mr. Davis,
tries to make it seem like it is not work.

"Washin' clothes is a game," she tells us.
"You just have to see how fast you can go,
and the first one done is the winner."

And though Miss Velma's voice is kind
and she laughs lightly when she says this,
it cannot be a game because
no matter how fast we work,
no matter how hard we work,
we are never done,
and so she is wrong
because there is never a winner.

"But we are never done," I tell her.

She laughs again as she folds the sheets
and shakes her head from side to side
as though I had told a funny story,
and when she laughs she reminds me
of Berta Smoke, who came to help
with our washing when my mother died,
except Miss Velma is not old.

"No, you are right. We are never done,"
she says. "But since it must be done,
we must make the most of it."

When I ask her what *make the most of it*
means, her laughter fades and she stares
toward the window as though she could see
something far in the distance, and when she
speaks her voice is soft and quiet,
and she reminds me of my mother.

"It means working in a laundry
because you have nowhere else to go."

"Why do you not go home?" I ask.

I cannot go home.
Home is too far and I am a child.
But Miss Velma is not a child.

She lifts her left hand
and brushes a loose strand of hair
away from her forehead as she turns toward me.

"I guess this is my home now," she answers.
and after a brief pause, she adds, smiling,
"I have to make my way in the world."

Her words echo those I heard from Mrs. Dwyer,
who said we must learn so we can improve
ourselves and make our way in the world.

I asked Mattie what it meant—
to make our way in the world.

But she did not know.

I do not know how washing clothes
will help me make my way in the world.

I would ask Miss Velma what it means,
but she is once more folding sheets.

mattie

Dear Father,

My teacher said I might write you
to tell you about the school
and how good we are being
here at school.

I am very happy.
I have a friend.
Her name is Gracie.

Sarah is happy, too.
She is being very good
and tries hard to learn her lessons.
She never complains
and has not cried.

You do not need to worry about us
because there are many people
who help us and take care of us.
The teachers here are all very nice,
and the matron who is like a mother
here at the school is very kind.

Sarah likes Mr. Davis very much.
He helps to keep the school clean.
She also likes Miss Velma, who runs
the laundry where Sarah works.

I like Miss Weston. She is the teacher
who told me I could write to you.

She said it would help my English.
She says I write very well.

We study hard and follow the rules.
We are trying to be good.
I think you would be proud of us.

Thank you for sending us to this school.

Your daughter,
Mattie

"What did you tell him?" Sarah asks.

I fold the paper carefully
so it will fit in the envelope
that Miss Weston gave me.

She will mail my letter
in the morning.

"I told him about the school,
and I told him about you.
I told him you were being very good,"
I tell her.

"You are, aren't you?" I ask.

"Let me see," she demands loudly,
reaching across the table for the paper.

"Don't you believe me?" I snap,
clutching the letter to my chest,

staring into Sarah's eyes,
defying her to question
my truthfulness.

"Would I lie to Father?"

Sarah pulls her arms back
and plants her elbows
on the table's wooden surface.

As she settles her face
sadly into her cupped hands,
she releases a long, quiet sigh.

"Did you tell him I want to come home?"

"No, I did not," I answer
in the strongest no-nonsense,
older-sister tone I can employ.
"Do you think Father wants to hear that?"

Her eyes begin to water
and I pretend not to see.

Instead, I smooth the folds of the paper,
running the tips of my fingers
back and forth, back and forth
along the creased edges.

"I told him you were being good,
that you are studying hard,
and that you never cry."

She looks up,

and with the cuff of her sleeve,
she dabs at the edges of her eyes.

"You did?"

I glance down at the letter.
I dare not look at my sister.

"Would I lie?"

sarah

My feet are tired of marching everywhere.
Like soldiers we march up and down
and down and up and across the yard.

We march to our meals and to our lessons
and to our work and to the church service
every Sunday morning and Wednesday night.

My feet are tired of marching everywhere.

Mrs. Dwyer stands at the end of the long row of beds,
rapping her ruler against the palm of her hand—
tap, tap, tap—as we exit for dinner.

"Let's go, girls. There is no time for chatter."

Far ahead of me in the line, I see Mattie,
arm in arm with Gracie Powless, as they
break stride and saunter toward the doorway,
Mattie whispering in Gracie's ear,
Gracie's eyes cast downward,
avoiding the scowl she must know is always
firmly frozen on Mrs. Dwyer's face,
Mattie's chin lifted upward in defiance.

Mattie will be in trouble again.

"Matilda Tarbell," Mrs. Dwyer barks. "Come here."

My sister is in trouble again.

Mattie slips her arm away from Gracie,
pushing her friend encouragingly forward
away from Mrs. Dwyer's wrath;
Gracie slips into step and marches on,
out the door, while my sister spins around
and stomps to attention.

"Perhaps we need to practice marching.
Perhaps we need practice more than dinner."

Mrs. Dwyer need not have included herself.
She never marches anywhere.

"I know how to march," Mattie answers sharply.

Mrs. Dwyer's ruler snaps sharply against
Mattie's cheek, and my heart leaps forward.

But I am not brave like Mattie.

My heart says to break rank and snatch the stick
out of Mrs. Dwyer's hand and save my sister.

But I do not.

I stay in line and wait for the signal
for us to continue our march past the scene
of will unfolding before us.

"Then march. Right here," Mrs. Dwyer says quietly,
but firmly, and as she waves her ruler back and forth
in front of her, she lifts her left hand,
signaling for the rest of us to continue out the door.

Mattie begins to march, but she goes nowhere.
Her feet move up and down, but she goes nowhere.

I want to look in her eyes as I file past,
but I do not dare to move my head in her direction.
I do not want to practice marching.

My feet are tired of marching everywhere.

Sometimes when we should be at lessons
or at work, Mattie pretends to be sick.
I think she is tired of marching everywhere, too.

I wish I was strong like Mattie;
I wish I was strong enough to help my sister,
but I do not want to feel Mrs. Dwyer's anger,
and I do not want to practice marching.

Mattie says my job is to be good.

I wonder what her job is.

MATTIE

Gracie Powless is my friend.
My very best friend.

Gracie is the most important person
in my life, except for Sarah.

Sarah is my sister,
and we will have each other forever.

But Gracie has no one.

I came to this place with Sarah.
Gracie came alone. She needs me.
So she is my best friend.

She is Onondaga and I am Mohawk
and so we are part of a great nation,
the HAUDENOSAUNEE,
and so we think and speak alike.

She is Bear Clan and so am I and so
she says that surely makes us sisters.

We both were sent to this school
because our families thought it best,
or at least they were told
it was our best chance.

Our best chance for what?

Mrs. Dwyer says if we work hard,
we will be as good as white people.
She says this is our chance to prove
we are as good as white people.

I may not always be good.

But Gracie is as good as anyone.

If coming to this school meant I met
Gracie, then I am glad I am here.

Gracie says I am her best friend.
She believes we would have
found each other anyway,
that we did not need a school
that makes us march everywhere.

Gracie does not like to march either.
She says it makes her feel as if
she is always in a hurry.
It makes her feel as though
her life is not real,
that her body marches off
while her soul stays behind.

Sometimes,
when our souls are together,
and we forget where we are,
we forget to march,
and then we are in trouble.
Again.

So here I am,
marching, going nowhere,
so I can prove to Mrs. Dwyer
that I know how to march.

I march and march and march,
going nowhere.

Mrs. Dwyer watches,
her arms folded across
the front of her black dress,
watching me march
and march and march,
going nowhere,
until Gracie and Sarah
and the other girls
march back from supper.

I do not mind missing supper.

I do not mind being in trouble.

But Gracie is not as strong as I am.
So I have to be strong for both of us.

saraн

Gracie will not look at me, will not look at me
scowling at her as we sit side by side at supper.

Gracie should have to practice marching, too.

I bet Mattie does not tell Gracie to be good.
I bet Mattie does not tell Gracie not to cry.

And I have seen Gracie cry.

I saw her cry when Miss Prentiss came to inspect
our beds and made Gracie make her bed again,
which was a foolish thing to cry about.

"You got my sister in trouble," I tell her.

Gracie's eyes grow wide.

"I wouldn't," she says. "She's my friend,
my very best friend."

"Then how come you are here?" I ask her.

I think I am hoping she will cry
so Mattie will not like her more than she likes me.

But when her eyes fill with water and she wipes
her sleeve across her face to keep the tears
from falling, I feel like crying, too.

MATTIE

"Matilda Tarbell,
what a terrible thing to say,"
Sarah exclaims, her hands
resting squarely on her hips.

If I wasn't so angry,
I would smile
because she looks
just like our mother did
when she would scold us
for arguing among ourselves
when we were little
and supposed to be at play.

But I am angry.

"Well, I do," I snap back,
tapping my fingers
on the top of the table
in the study room,
where I sit with my books before me.

"I hate Mrs. Dwyer," I repeat.

"What would Father think," she scolds,
looking around furtively
to see if anyone is listening,
"to hear you say something so mean?"

Father can be stern,

but he is a quiet person,
a kind person.

Yes, Sarah is right.
Father would be upset.

"Father is not here," I remind her.
"Are you going to write and tell him?"

I see her body lose its stiffness
as she considers my question.

"You have my permission,"
I offer grandly,
waving my right hand
lightly in the air.

"Go ahead. Write him," I say.

"Write and tell him that
Matilda Tarbell, his daughter,
is not being good," I add,
challenging Sarah,
knowing she will not.

"You should not hate anyone, Mattie,"
she says, her voice growing softer.

She slides into the chair across from me.

"Well, I don't care.
I never thought anyone hated me,"
I respond sharply.

I know I am cross
because I am ashamed
that I let my anger show,
ashamed that I let Mrs. Dwyer
make me feel mean.

And I do feel mean.

"Mattie?" Sarah whispers.
She leans forward as though
we were about to share a great secret.
"You do not really hate her, do you?"

Her deep, brown eyes look so sad.
I think she must be worrying
that I have put my soul
in great danger.

She should worry more about Mrs. Dwyer's.

"Oh, probably not really," I tell her,
trying to add some lightness
to the sound of my voice
as though I have shed the anger
that has firmly fixed itself
inside my heart.

"But I must say," I add,
"that I hope she steps in a hole
and is swallowed up by the earth."

Suddenly Sarah's eyes brighten
and a smile spreads across her face.

"Mattie, how dreadful," she says
in mock horror.

"What a terrible thing to do to Mother Earth."

sarah

The heat presses into my head,
and I long for the freshness of the wind which
sweeps along the river behind my father's house.

I do not think it can ever be my house again.

Mattie says maybe we will go home soon,
but I fear we will never go home again.

I wonder if anyone ever goes home.

The heat presses onto my face,
and I must breathe in deeply through my nose
to catch my breath.

I never used to think about breathing.

Yesterday I fell in a heap on the floor with the
unfolded sheet still in my hands, and I think
Miss Velma was more frightened than I was.

I was not sick.

I was hot,
so very, very hot,
and my body just melted onto the stone floor.

Miss Velma patted my face with a damp cloth,
but it wasn't cool like the cloth my mother put on
my forehead when I was little and had a great fever.

Miss Velma's cloth was hot and smelled stale.

"Sarah Tarbell, you scared me half to death,"
she chided sharply as I rose slowly to my feet,
her hand on my elbow.

And then she let me sit outside on the stone steps
long enough for me to close my eyes and dream of home,
where sheets draped over the line that stretches
from the back corner of the house to a post near the barn
dry quickly from our river's wind.

The sheets on my bed at home smell sweet and fresh
like the sweetgrass baskets my mother used to make.

School sheets smell stale even when they are clean,
and I know they are clean because I work in the laundry.

But I wish I did not.

It is hot and smells of dirty water and strong soap
and hot bodies that cannot breathe.

And so I sat on the stone steps catching my breath,
dreaming of home.

And before my dream was done,
a voice cracked sharply above my head,
and before I opened my eyes,
I knew the face that matched that voice.

"Just what are you doing out here?"
Mrs. Dwyer demanded.

I looked upward, shielding my eyes from the sun,
and saw her immense grayness looming over me,
hands on her hips, scowl on her face.

Mrs. Dwyer knows only how to scowl.

"I told her to sit there. She needed some air.
The laundry is very hot today."

The laundry is very hot every day.

Miss Velma's voice was quiet but firm,
and as I glanced over my shoulder to see
her standing in the doorway, her hands, too,
were on her hips, and though there was no
scowl on her face, there also was no smile.

"The laundry is hot for everyone. We all have
a responsibility here. If we pamper one child,
we will end up pampering them all," Mrs. Dwyer
scolded, each word spoken deliberately, her tone
implying that nothing else need be said.

"I allowed the child some fresh air," Miss Velma
explained in exasperated tones. "She had fainted."

I studied my shoes, afraid to lift my face.
Mrs. Dwyer would think I pretended to be sick.

I do not pretend to be sick.
But sometimes I think Mattie does
when she does not want to wake up.
And Mrs. Dwyer knows Mattie is my sister.

"Get back inside," Mrs. Dwyer demanded.

I glanced up slightly to see if her sharp words were
directed toward me, and when our eyes met,
I knew they were.

I rose from the steps and moved inside,
and I did not look at Miss Velma when I brushed
past her skirt.

And it is so hot again today and the heat presses
into my face, and Miss Velma is not here to save me
if I fall in a heap on the floor.

MATTIE

Poor Sarah.

She cried herself to sleep tonight,
but I can't be angry with her.

If she were crying for home,
I might understand.

If she were longing
for our mother and father,
I might understand.

But she is crying
because Miss Velma is leaving.

Poor Sarah.

"Miss Velma was nice," she said to me.
"She let me sit on the steps and breathe.
It was almost like sitting on the porch
at home with mother when she said
it was too hot in the kitchen."

"Miss Velma is not our mother," I told her.

Then she cried some more
and buried her face into her pillow,
while I sat on the edge of her bed
and patted her shoulder.

But I cannot take away the hurt.

I am not her mother either.

At supper Ida sent whisperings
around the dining hall.
She said Miss Velma was in trouble
because she disobeyed Mrs. Dwyer
and that it was all Sarah's fault.

I told her to hush.

But she wouldn't.

We watched after supper
as Miss Velma drove away
in the wagon with Mr. Davis.
Mr. Davis had strapped
a brown valise in place behind her,
and I wondered if
the contents of her whole world
were packed tightly inside it.

Sarah wanted to run outside
to say good-bye,
but I wouldn't let her,
and so she cried again,
and I couldn't be angry with her.

"Why is Miss Velma going away?"
Sarah asked through her tears though
I knew she did not need the answer.

They sent Miss Velma away
because she was nice.

saraн

I thought I was dying.

When I undressed for bed and saw the stains,
I thought my body was punishing me
for sending Miss Velma away.

Mattie says it is why I fell in a heap
on the floor of the laundry.

She says I am becoming a woman.

I do not want to be a woman
if it means falling in a heap on the floor
and having Mrs. Dwyer scold more and more
and having Miss Velma go away.

When I told Mattie not to tell anyone,
she put her arms around me and leaned
her head against mine and said nothing.

When I asked Mattie how long I would
have to be a woman, she whispered,
"Forever."

But I am not a woman;
I am not a woman because I
cried and cried and cried like a little child.

MATTIE

Poor Sarah.

"Mattie, come here,"
she called quietly
as we were hurrying
to ready for bed before
the lights went out.

"Look," she said
as she pointed secretly
to the dark stains
on her undergarments.

Her stricken face told me
she thought she was dying.

"Oh," I replied,
trying to sound unconcerned,
"is that all?"

"What does it mean, Mattie?
Am I dying?"

"Oh, no," I told her.

"It's probably why you fainted
in the laundry," I explained,
trying to assure her she was not dying.
"It means you are becoming a woman.
It means you will be able to have babies."

I hope I will have babies someday.

I have not been a woman
since we came to school.
I had been a woman at home.

I should have been a woman
two times since we left home.
No one knows, not even Sarah,
and I don't know why I am not.

My mother was so proud
when I became a woman,
so very, very proud that
she made a special basket
just for me, a basket made of
sweetgrass and blue-dyed black ash.
She said it was only for me
and I should keep
womanly thoughts in it.

When I asked her
what were womanly thoughts,
she told me I would know
when I had them.

I left my basket at home.
Perhaps I will become a woman again
when I return.

"What do I do?" Sarah asked.

"I can show you," I answered.

"Please, Mattie, do not tell anyone,"
she pleaded softly.

I put my arms around her
and leaned my head against hers
and said nothing.

Then she asked me how long
she would have to be a woman.

"Forever," I told her.

And then she cried.

saraн

"Sarah?"

In the distant corners of my mind I hear the voice of my mother
as she stands on the wooden steps, calling me in to supper.
I see her hands cupped around the edges of her mouth,
calling out toward the banks of our great river,
where I sit at its edge on my favorite stone,
letting the water, cold even in the heat of summer,
flow in and out around my feet.

"Saaaaarraah . . ."

Ake'nistenha

Mother

But it is not my mother who calls my name.

And the hardness under my body is not a massive
stone that has felt the river flowing against it
since longer than even before my grandmother was born.

"Sarah. Pay attention, please."

It is Miss Weston who calls my name,
Miss Weston who stands in the front of the classroom,
her hands clutching the sides of her book.

"It is your turn to read," she says.

"I have lost my place," I tell her quietly,
looking up in time to see her shoulders sag
as she sighs and shakes her head from side to side.

"Really, Sarah, you must remember to follow along
when others are reading, " she tells me.

I do not remember who was reading,
and I do not remember what was being read.

I only remember the sound of the river's waves
as they lapped against the rocks;
I only remember the sound of the wind
as it pushed the water forward to the shore;
I only remember my mother's voice
rising and falling as it flew on the wind,
calling me home.

I do not remember who was reading,
or what was being read.

I cannot remember everything.

I feel my cheeks grow warm,
and as the water rises in my eyes,
I tell myself that I must remember not to cry.

I am no longer a child who can cry for her mother.

I must remember that I am now a woman.

MATTIE

"But Miss Prentiss said
I should bring these to you,"
I told Mrs. Dwyer this morning
as I pointed to the pile of mending
I had placed neatly
on the small oak table by the window.

"Students are not allowed in here,"
she repeated,
the lines of her forehead deepening
as her black eyes glared at me,
her hands planted firmly on her hips.

"I'm sorry," I said,
"but the door was open
so I thought—"

But what I thought
did not matter to Mrs. Dwyer,
who would not let me finish.

"—thought that it was acceptable
to enter where one does not belong. . . ."
she finished for me.

"Miss Prentiss said you
needed these," I explained,
pointing to the clothes which lay
on the table near the window
as starched and pressed and stiff
as Mrs. Dwyer.

"Did Miss Prentiss tell you
to enter if I was not here?"

"She said I was to hurry,
to bring you your mending,"
I said, pointing again
to the pile on the table,
"and the door was open
so I thought—"

But Mrs. Dwyer,
who does not listen,
would not let me finish
and, instead, stared,
stared fiercely into my face.

"I never leave my door open,"
she barked harshly.
"Lying is unacceptable, Matilda."

She brushed past me, muttering
something about Indians
not knowing the difference
between truth and lying,
and I felt my cheeks grow hot
because I know the difference
between truth and lying
and I know Indians who do not
and I know white people who do not.

"I'm not lying," I said to her back
as she stood beside the table
and ran her fingers
lightly across the garments

I had mended as though
she were smoothing out creases
that could not possibly have been there.

"I knocked on your door," I continued,
"and you didn't answer.
I tried the door and it was open
and so I came in,
but just to leave your things,
just to leave them
like Miss Prentiss said I should."

"When a door is closed," she said,
each word spoken slowly
as she turned to face me,
each word spoken louder
than the word before it,
"it is not open."

Then she sighed deeply,
as though she were so very tired,
and after a long pause,
when she spoke again,
her words came streaming
quickly through her clenched teeth.

"If no one answers
when you knock at a door,
you do not just walk in.
You return later."

Return later?
But I had her clothes.
Return later?

When her door was open?
Why would I do this?

At home, at AKWESASNE,
no one is this silly.
Our doors are always open.
People are always welcome.

If my mother had a gift of food
for neighbors and found
they were not at home,
she would not leave it on the stoop
or on the steps or on the porch
where someone's pet might help itself.
Instead, she left it on the stove
or by the hearth
or on the kitchen table
to be quickly found
when they returned.

When my father cut a load of wood
for Berta Smoke, whose husband
broke his leg one winter
when he fell upon the ice
just outside their barn,
we did not stop to see
if they were there
before we stacked it
beside the back steps
and filled the empty woodbox
just inside the door.

And when we passed them
on the road coming from town,

their dark mules
plodding heavily along,
Father did not stop to tell them
where we'd been
and what we'd done.

He waved silently
and only later learned
that Berta had taken Henry
all the way to town
to have the cast removed.

"I'm sorry," I told her again.

But she said nothing.

Instead, she shook her head
from side to side
and waved her left hand
in the air toward me,
signaling me to go.

There was nothing more to be said.

So I turned and left the room,
hearing the click of the door
as it closed quickly behind me,
hearing the snap of the bolt
as it locked in place,
hearing Mrs. Dwyer in my head
saying that, indeed,
her door was closed.

sarah

"You do?" I ask Mattie,
who sits on the edge of her bed,
her arms wrapped around herself.
"You want to go home?"

Mattie has told me over and over
that I must be brave, that I must be good,
that Father expects us to be good,
that we cannot go home.

And now Mattie wants to go home,
and I am surprised
because I am the one who still cries at night
when I hope no one is listening.

I am the one who wants to go home.

Mattie turns quickly, looking over her shoulder at me,
and then slowly, calmly rises from the bed
with a look on her face that tells me her thoughts
were not meant for my ears.

"Don't be silly," she says lightly.
"We're not going home."

"I heard you," I tell her. "I heard what you said."

"You heard wrong," she says
in her usual bossy Mattie way.

"Don't you miss our home?" I ask her.

"Don't you miss Father?"

"We have much to learn. We can't do that at home,"
she explains, her words echoing what we hear
from Miss Weston, from Miss Prentiss, from Mrs. Dwyer.

She says the words, but the sound of her voice betrays her.

I know my sister.

I know when she is bossy and mean and proud,
and I know when she is sad.

"Mattie," I whisper as I move close to her
so no one else can hear my secret,
so no one else will see what I want to show her.

I have caught her attention.

"What is it?" she asks, whispering, too,
looking around to see who might be listening.

"Come, come see," I say as I take her hand
and lead her toward my bureau.

I open the bottom drawer and pull out
the scarf that Mother made for me,
the scarf that Father let me bring to school
even though we were told everything,
everything we would need, would be here,
that we need not bring anything from home.

I sit down on the edge of the bed,
holding this bundle of woven material in my lap,

and slowly, carefully, unfold the edges,
watching Mattie as keenly as a hawk,
all the while holding my breath.

"What do you have there?" she asks impatiently.

"Shh," I warn her, looking around.

As the edges of the scarf fall open,
Mattie's hands fly to her mouth.

"Ooooh, my basket, my beautiful basket,"
she says as she drops onto the bed next to me.
"Sarah, you have my basket,"
she tells me as though I do not know.

So many weeks ago, when we were packing
the few things we would bring to school,
I saw Mattie looking longingly at her basket,
setting it on the table with the items we wanted to take
until Father came in to check our progress and shook his head
and said no, there was no need to take her basket.
And when he left the room, Mattie's shoulders shook,
and even though she made no sound,
I heard the tears in her heart.

"Father let me bring my scarf," I tell her.
"He should have let you bring your basket."
And I find myself smiling smugly,
knowing Father has likely not noticed that
Mattie's basket is missing from the table beside our bed,
knowing I have taken Mattie's sadness
and lifted it from her heart.

As my sister sits beside me on this bed that is not our bed,
in this place that is not our home,
her shoulders begin to shake,
and even though she makes no sound,
I hear the tears of joy in her heart.

MATTIE

"Mrs. Dwyer better not see that,"
Gracie chides as I proudly show her
my basket.

"She won't see it," I assure her.

I told Sarah
that I had to show Gracie
my beautiful basket,
but I promised her
that I would show no one else,
that I would hide it
beneath my nightclothes
in the bottom of my bureau.

But I had to show Gracie my basket.

"If Mrs. Dwyer sees it,
you will be in trouble."

Gracie does not need to tell me that.

Mrs. Dwyer made it very clear that,
while we may have things from home,
under no circumstances were we to have
Indian things from home.

"She won't see it,"
I tell Gracie confidently
as I hold it up so she can admire
my mother's work.

"Isn't it beautiful?" I add,
expecting her to agree as I finger
the woven piece of blue-dyed black ash
that the unskilled eye,
from a distance,
often thinks is ribbon.

"It is," she answers.

My basket is not very large.
If I hold my hands together,
palms up,
it will fit inside
the outside edges of my hands.

My mother made many baskets,
many larger than mine,
but the one she made for me
is just the right size
because Sarah
was able to hide it
in our satchel
and in her bureau
so she could give it to me
when I needed it most,
when I needed something,
something from home,
and because it is not too big,
I, too, can now hide it,
can keep it safe,
in my bottom drawer.

"And smell," I say,
pulling it close to my nose

and inhaling deeply,
then offering it to Gracie
so she, too, can smell
the sweetness of the dried grass.

She holds my basket to her nose
and nods agreeably
but then quickly returns it to my hands.

"You'd better put it away,"
she says nervously,
looking over her shoulder
toward the door
as the sound of voices
in the hallway grows.

Her words are wise,
but I have a plan to protect
my mother's gift
should someone see it
who might think
I should not have it.

I will pretend
it means nothing,
just a simple place
to hold pins and thread
and needles and stray buttons.

Even Gracie, who is my best friend,
does not know how special it is.

Only Sarah and I know
how special it is,

and only I know now
how special Sarah is
to have brought my basket
to school for me.

So now my basket
will also be Sarah's,
for Sarah has no mother now
to make her one,
and together we will share
this special place
to keep our womanly thoughts.

sarah

We splash through the puddles on the path
that leads from the dining hall to the classrooms
and fling open the door, laughing at the rain
that caught us all by surprise.

The Thunder Beings have saved us from marching.

Even Ruthie is smiling today.

But Miss Weston is not smiling.
She stands in the hall,
her hands thrown in the air.

"My goodness, you will all be sick,"
she exclaims as we shake our bodies
just like our dogs at home that shed the water
from their swim in the St. Regis, where
they go because the great river is too strong
even for their sturdy bodies.

Even Ruthie, who comes from where there
is very little rain and no great river
like our mighty St. Lawrence, even Ruthie
shakes her head and shoulders and laughs.

I have never heard Ruthie laugh.

Just then the Thunderers roar from the sky
and Miss Weston throws her hands up once more.

"It's only the Grandfathers, Miss Weston,"
Mattie explains. "No need to be afraid."

"Oh my goodness, I certainly am not afraid,
not afraid of a little storm," she says loudly
as she ushers us into the classroom.

But the shaking of her voice says she is afraid,
and Ruthie and I exchange glances,
hiding our laughter behind our eyes.

I think Ruthie feels like I do,
pleased that our teacher, for once,
is afraid of something that we are not.

"Come, come, children," she says.
"Sit down. Let's begin our lessons."

But the Thunder Beings shout out once more,
and Miss Weston drops the paper in her hand,
and Ruthie and I cannot hide our laughter.

"Oh my goodness," she says again.
"Will it never end?"

"The thunder is good, Miss Weston," Mattie tells her
quietly, calmly, casting scolding eyes at me
for laughing at the only teacher she likes.

"It brings the rain," she adds, picking up the paper
that drifted gently to the floor and placing it on the desk.

Mattie can cast scolding eyes at me all day long.

I do not care.

I hope it rains and rains and rains all day.
Then we will have to run instead of march.

MATTIE

Gracie and I sit
side by side on the steps
that lead up to the porch
of our dormitory.

The day is unusually warm
for late October
and the sun's rays
shine brightly on our faces.

Gracie and I sit
side by side on the steps,
holding our breath,
holding in our laughter
as we listen to the conversation
coming from the open window.

"What makes you think
you can convince Mrs. Dwyer
that you should be captain?"
we hear one of the older girls say.

"Miss Prentiss likes me,"
a shrill voice answers,
a voice that I think is Ida's.
"I will ask Miss Prentiss
to speak to Mrs. Dwyer for me.
She will, too.
Miss Prentiss knows
she can count on me."

"Count on you for what?"
the other voice asks.

"Well, I don't know yet.
For whatever she needs.
And if she can count on me,
then I can count on her."

"Count on her for what?"
the second voice asks.

"Well, I don't know yet.
But you never know,
you never know
when being able
to count on someone,
someone like Miss Prentiss,
just might be helpful," Ida explains,
sounding even more pompous
than Ida usually sounds.

"I don't know why you
want to be captain, anyway,"
says the voice I cannot identify.
"Nobody will like you."

The voice I do not know is right.
I do not know why anyone
would want to be captain,
lining us up to march
off to lessons and work,
acting as helpers for our matron
when she and Miss Prentiss
are elsewhere with their duties,

being the person in power,
for the moment,
that many of us will not like.

Not that I like Ida anyway.

"I don't care who likes me,"
Ida says,
"as long as Mrs. Dwyer
and Miss Prentiss do.
Besides, Mrs. Dwyer
should have made me captain
a long time ago,
and now that Alice
has been sent
to work in the city,
I have my chance."

Gracie places her hands
on her hips
and moves her elbows
back and forth,
back and forth,
while she moves her mouth
without making a sound,
mocking the image
we both have in our heads
of Ida asserting herself
to impress her friend.

I cover my mouth
to hide my laughter,
and shake a finger at Gracie,
pretending to scold.

We are being naughty.
We should not be listening.

But we are.

We hear the second voice again.

"Mrs. Dwyer," she says,
"will choose her captain carefully.
You might need more help
than Miss Prentiss can give."

"Oh, I have more help than Miss Prentiss,"
Ida says, her voice strong and confident.
"Miss Prentiss will open the door for me,
but I can take care of the rest."

"How will you do that?"
the other voice asks.

"I have my ways," Ida adds darkly,
emphasizing each word.
"I have my ways."

Ida's curious tone
sends shivers through me
and as I look at Gracie,
I see in her eyes that she, too,
has heard the eeriness
in Ida's haunting words.

I wish we had not listened.

saraн

"Matilda Tarbell!"

Mrs. Dwyer's voice rings sharply, strongly,
throughout the dormitory,
and I know Mattie must be in trouble.

I look quickly at Mattie, who has risen
to her feet, and her eyes tell me she knows
she is in trouble, but her mouth hung open and
her chin dropped low tells me she does not know why.

Mattie's face is not good at lying.

Mrs. Dwyer stands in the doorway,
her ruler slapping against the palm of her left hand
as she calls out to Mattie once more.

"Matilda! Come here!"

Mrs. Dwyer's voice has moved angrily across the room
and Mattie's usual defiance creeps under her bed
as she moves forward slightly, cautiously.

"Well?" this angry woman demands.

Mattie looks up but does not answer.

"What has she done?" I ask for my sister,
surprised that Mattie does not respond,
for Mattie always has something to say,
surprised at myself for speaking to Mrs. Dwyer at all.

Mrs. Dwyer's head turns sharply toward me,
and I find myself instinctively shrinking inward,
startled by the blaze of hate.
For when I see her eyes, burning like the glowing coals
that remained for days and days after a fire
swept through my grandmother's log home,
I know why Mattie says nothing.

"Quiet!" she commands.

As I look for support among our sister students,
their heads bow in fear, and only Gracie's eyes
meet mine momentarily before she, too,
begins to examine the making of her bed.

"This is not your business," Mrs. Dwyer adds,
and then turns her angry face back to my sister,
whose eyes are on me,
whose eyes are telling me to be quiet.

"Where is it?" Mrs. Dwyer demands.

"What?" Mattie asks weakly,
her eyes returning this woman's fiery glare
not with anger but with confusion.

"You know very well *what*," she offers in explanation,
which Mattie's face shows is clearly no explanation at all.

Mattie's face does not lie,
and so I do not need to know *what*
to know that she did not do whatever
Mrs. Dwyer thinks she did.

"Return it now and show repentance," she says stiffly,
"and your punishment will be less.
But if your stubbornness should prevail,
then I will be forced to handle this matter with severity."

And for the first time since this woman
who handles everything with severity
has entered the room, Mattie becomes herself.

"I don't know what you are looking for."

And perhaps the defiance that has returned
to Mattie's face and voice is her undoing,
for in five long, but rapid, steps Mrs. Dwyer
crosses the room to where Mattie stands
and pauses for only a moment before a loud crack echoes
as she smacks her stick across my sister's face.

"No-o-o," I cry, hurrying to Mattie,
who has fallen backward onto her bed.

I rush around the end of the beds
that separate me from Mattie,
but before I can reach my sister's side,
Mrs. Dwyer's long black sleeve wraps around my waist
and pulls me away, away from my sister,
who sits on the edge of her bed rubbing her cheek.

"Perhaps this *is* your business,"
Mrs. Dwyer says as her right hand grabs my arm,
turning me around so that we are face-to-face,
her purple face dark and scowling,
mine hot and wet with tears.

"Perhaps you know very well what
your sister has done," she continues.

"Leave her alone," Mattie shouts angrily,
rising to her feet, hands now clenched at her sides,
a harsh red mark already swelling on her dark skin.
"We don't know what you are talking about."

"We shall see about that," Mrs. Dwyer answers.

She releases her grip on my arm and pushes me,
and then Mattie, out of her way as she begins to search,
easily lifting the thin mattress of Mattie's bed,
sliding her hand all around the inside of the pillow cover,
moving the few items Mattie keeps on top of the bureau
as though what she looked for was lurking
behind a hairbrush or a propped-up book.

Mattie comes and stands beside me,
and through the touch of her arm
around my shoulder I sense the fear she feels
as Mrs. Dwyer snaps open each drawer
and lifts Mattie's clothes in bunches
as she gropes around the insides of the bureau,
and when she slams shut the bottom drawer,
Mattie's arm falls limply to my side.

Mrs. Dwyer turns sharply and glares at us,
and then moves, without a word,
to where I sleep, where she repeats her search,
while we all stand in silence,
wondering and waiting.

When her searching is done, and whatever it is

she was searching for is not found,
she returns to Mattie's bureau and picks up her ruler
and steps back into the space between the two rows of beds
that line the walls of the room, where she stands,
slapping the ruler—*snap, snap, snap*—
sharply into the palm of her left hand,
while we all stand in silence,
wondering and waiting.

She breathes in and out deeply,
the only person in the room who is breathing at all,
and her eyes move around the room slowly, but stiffly,
from one frightened girl to another,
and when she speaks,
she speaks slowly, carefully, coldly.

"A very important possession of mine . . ."
She pauses and looks around the room once more.
". . . has been stolen." She pauses again.
"And one person, one person in this room,
had the access and, most likely, the inclination
since she constantly defies my position
and my desire to see that you are all
given the opportunity to improve yourselves."

She pauses once more,
but now she looks directly at Mattie.

"But some young ladies are too arrogant
and think they do not need to improve themselves.
Some young ladies think they know what is best for themselves . . .
which, I assure you, they do not."

Again, she pauses, her eyes centering on Mattie,

and the silence in the room is so strong that
when she speaks again, I hear my heart jump.

"Someone must know something," she says quietly
as she looks once more from girl to girl,
each one dropping her eyes to the floor
if they had not been there already.

"Keeping important information from me,
information that could help to return my silver brooch . . ."
She pauses and draws her breath in through her teeth
so sharply that a hissing sound is heard.
". . . is the same as . . . stealing."

At the mention of the silver brooch,
a thick, heavy piece of gray metal with curved edges,
I cannot help but glance at the front of her dress,
where we often saw it pinned just beneath her left shoulder
and I wonder why she thinks Mattie,
or anyone, would want something so ugly.

". . . and the punishment for stealing, and lying,
is not to be taken lightly," she continues.
"So . . . should someone remember something,
I suggest she come to see me . . . soon."

And with those words, she turns and
stomps across the room and through the door.

And now there is a silence that echoes endlessly
throughout the room as all eyes stare at my sister,
who kneels before her bureau, pawing desperately
at the clothes in disarray in the bottom drawer.

Mattie

RAKE'NIHA

Father

You want me to be good.
You want me to learn.
It's too hard to be good, Father.
It's too hard to be good here.

The room is so quiet
I hear no one breathing,
and I feel the eyes
of my sister students
staring at me, wondering.

She has brought me shame.
She has brought my sister shame.
She has brought my family shame.

What shall I do?

saraн

"No, I did not take her pin," Mattie says.

I believe her.
I can look at Mattie's face
and see that she tells the truth.

Mattie's face is not good at lying.

"Why does she say it is you?" asks Ruthie,
whose face says she does not know Mattie
as well as I do.

"She hates me," Mattie answers.

"She hates everyone," Gracie offers softly
from where she sits on the edge of her own bed.

"Would she make it up?" Ruthie asks.

"My sister does not lie," I shout,
glaring at Ruthie, who I thought was my friend,
glaring at Gracie, whose words seem like
a weak defense for her friend.

"She might," Mattie says, lifting her chin in the air
as she nods her head toward Ruthie.
"I tell you, she hates me."

Ruthie stands at the foot of my sister's bed,
shaking her head in disagreement.
"No," she says. "She was too angry."

"Well, I didn't take it," Mattie replies sharply.

Many pairs of eyes stare at us, Mattie and I,
as we sit side by side on her bed,
many pairs of eyes silently asking the question,
wondering if Mattie is telling the truth,
while I wonder how they can think she is not.

"Do you believe Mrs. Dwyer?" I ask of all
who have gathered near my sister's bed.
"Do you think my sister is a thief?"

Some girls shake their heads back and forth,
showing support for my sister,
while several others shrug their shoulders,
and return to their own spaces in the room.

But Ida,
who some think should be in a room
on the first floor with the older girls,
who Mattie said was probably on our floor
so she could tell Mrs. Dwyer when we did not follow the rules,
puts her hands on her waist and glowers at Mattie,
and at first I think she might be making fun,
trying to look like Mrs. Dwyer,
but when she speaks, there is a sharpness in her voice
that cuts through me like the wind off the river in winter.

"Just maybe she is," Ida says.
"She hates Mrs. Dwyer. I heard her say so.
Maybe she did take her pin. Just to upset her."

"Not true," I shout, trying not to cry.
"Mattie would not do that."

I know my sister.
I know my sister does not lie.
I know my sister would not steal.

"Well, if she didn't take it, who did?" Ida demands,
looking around, daring anyone to return her glare.

"Who did?" she asks again when she is met with silence.
"You heard Mrs. Dwyer. Do we want her angry at us?
Should we be blamed for something someone else did?"

"I didn't take it," Mattie says quietly,
but with a firmness in her voice that says
she is offended by Ida's accusation.

"Well, how do we know that's the truth," Ida asks.

"I know it's the truth," Mattie answers.
"I don't care what you think."

"I believe her," Gracie says.

She moves from her bed to Mattie's
and sits down beside her and puts her arm
around my sister and pats her gently in comfort,
and I am grateful that Gracie is Mattie's friend.

Mattie

RAKE'NIHA

Father

How can I stay here?

sarah

Keepers of the Eastern Door.

That is what my grandmother told me a long, long time ago
when I was a little child and would sit on a stool
beside her kitchen table, helping her husk the corn
as she prepared to make soup.

She said I must always remember that we,
the **KANIEN'KEHAKA,** the Mohawk people,
are Keepers of the Eastern Door,
and that long ago it was through us
that people were allowed to travel the lands
of the **HAUDENOSAUNEE,** the Iroquois;
and we allowed all to pass through our lands,
as long as we knew they traveled in peace.

I look at the wooden door where
Mrs. Dwyer has passed through.

I wish I could be
the Keeper of the Eastern Door here
and only let those enter who wish to come
in peace.

MATTIE

"Did you ask her?"
Sarah whispers to me
as we pass by each other
in the dining hall.

She thought maybe
Gracie had taken
my basket from my drawer,
had taken it to admire
or to show one of the girls.

I knew Gracie would not
do that without asking,
but I told Sarah I would ask
even though I feared Gracie
would be hurt to think
I could not trust her
with a secret.

"She doesn't know,"
I tell Sarah, confident
that I tell her the truth,
"and I believe her."

"Then where is it?"

I have no answer.

I had hoped that
it was Sarah who had
taken my beautiful basket.

But it wasn't.

And it wasn't Gracie.

Sarah said ask, ask everyone
if someone had seen my basket.

Sarah was so sure
that the person who took
Mrs. Dwyer's pin
probably took my basket.

But I did not dare to ask.

I would have to tell
the truth about my basket.

Sarah does not see
that sometimes
the truth does not matter.

saraн

"Sarah! Please pay attention," Miss Weston scolds.

She sounds cross and I do not care.

I cannot pay attention.

I cannot study.

I cannot learn.

I can only think about Mattie, who, for three days,
has not been allowed to go to her classes.

Mattie has spent three whole days with Miss Prentiss,
sewing and mending and sewing and mending.

She says Miss Prentiss says that Mrs. Dwyer says
that working all day will give her time to think,
to think about doing the right thing,
but when we have time together in the evening after dinner,
when whispering voices have crept into the corners of the night,
Mattie is too tired to talk, which is probably a good thing
because if we talked too much I would tell her
how some of the girls, especially the older ones,
point at me and whisper behind their cupped hands.

But I know Mattie's heart must be hurting
because Mattie likes learning
and she especially likes Miss Weston.

But I don't.

"Sarah! Come to the board, please."

I slide out from my desk and move to the front of the room.

Miss Weston hands me a piece of chalk.

"Write two nouns that you see in the room,"
she commands, nodding toward the chalkboard.

When I do not move, she puts her hands on her hips and asks,
"You do remember what a noun is, don't you?"

No, I do not remember.

I look around the classroom slowly,
searching for some help in the faces that stare back at me,
but no one's eyes tell me about nouns.

"Only two, Sarah. Certainly you can identify two nouns,"
Miss Weston urges, her voice sounding more tired than cross.
"Just look around the room and write down what you see."

I look around the room once more and then turn to face the board.

I lift the piece of chalk high above my head,
and with Mattie's voice in my memory telling me to write carefully,
I slowly draw the letters I see forming in my mind.

FEER

SOROW

"Are those nouns?" I ask Miss Weston softly
as I place the chalk back into the tray beneath the board,
wondering if I should return to my desk.

She does not answer for a long time, and I think she
must be angry because I do not know my nouns,
but it does not matter because I do not care
because I cannot think about nouns right now.

I can only think about Mattie.

"Yes, Sarah, those are nouns," she says.

MATTIE

"Psst . . . Gracie," I whisper softly
but strongly as I stand beside her bed,
urging her to wake up.

She turns restlessly under the covers
and I shake her shoulder lightly.

"Gracie," I whisper again.
"Wake up."

Gracie and I have a plan,
and we must go now,
past the peak of night,
yet hours before the dawn,
a time chosen carefully,
cautiously, hopefully,
to avoid the shadows of the moon
and to escape the unfair accusations
that shame me and my family.

Get up, I shout to myself.
Get up, Gracie.

Mrs. Dwyer shamed me
and said I stole her brooch,
and now, besides Sarah,
it is only Gracie
who will speak to me
and sit with me.

The other students are such cowards.

When Mrs. Dwyer's word
spread throughout the school,
even the boys,
even those who make faces
when Mrs. Dwyer speaks to all,
would not speak to me
or even look in my direction.

They are all cowards.

Sarah says they are not;
she says they are afraid,
and when I asked her
if there is a difference,
she said there is,
but I told her being afraid
when you can see the truth
makes no sense.

So when I told Gracie
I was leaving,
Gracie said she was not afraid,
that she would go with me.
Then she asked where I was going
and I told her I was going home.

ᴀᴋᴡᴇꜱᴀꜱɴᴇ

But I cannot go home.

I cannot go home to my father
who told me to be good.
I cannot bring him shame.
For though I know he will believe me

when I tell him that I did not steal,
the look in his eyes that will come
when he learns I could not be good,
that I did not take care of my sister,
that I left her to be good by herself,
will be more than I can bear.

So how can I go home?

Gracie said we could go
to her grandmother's,
that her grandmother
would understand,
that her grandmother
would take us in,
that her grandmother
did not want Gracie to go
to the Indian school,
that she would persuade
Gracie's mother and father
to let us stay with her.

But now Gracie will not get up.

"Gracie," I hiss in her ear.
"Wake up."

But she will not wake up.

She rolls over in her bed
and pulls the blanket
up over her head,
and I wonder if she, too,
like the others, is afraid,

and I wonder if I can find
her grandmother
by myself.

I look across the row of beds
to where Sarah lies sleeping.

Sarah would wake
with a single touch to her shoulder.
I could put my finger to my lips
and she would say nothing.
She would rise and dress silently
and come with me
and question nothing
because she is my sister.

I look down, once more, at Gracie,
who breathes so deeply I wonder
if she is pretending to be asleep,
and now I know that there are journeys
one must take alone.

I turn and step soundlessly
out of the room.

saraн

I sit on the edge of my bed,
feeling the chill of the early morning,
and I am puzzled by what I see,
or rather what I do not see.

Mattie is not in her bed.

I am always awake before Mattie.

I sit on the edge of my bed and stare,
and my heart begins to beat wildly.

Mattie is not in her bed,
and her bed is not made.

MATTIE

It was so dark
I could hardly find my way
through the hole in the fence
by the old stone gates
that marked the entrance
to the school a long time ago.

It is here where the railroad tracks
lie closest to the edge of the school,
where the tracks go one way into town
and the other way toward home.

If I were bigger or stronger or faster,
I might have climbed the train
that moved north in the night.

But even though it moved slowly,
I was not big enough
or strong enough
or fast enough to board the train
that might have taken me home.

Home is so far, so so far away,
but if I can march and march
to work and school and supper,
then I can walk to my home.

And I got through the fence.

For once I am glad my body is small,
so small that squeezing

through the hole in the fence
was possible once I found the place.

Sarah could not have
fit through the fence.

Gracie might have,
if she would have come.
And if she had,
we would have gone together,
to be with her grandmother,
and though her grandmother
might welcome me alone,
I don't even know her name,
and I don't know where to find her.

But Gracie's fear
would not let her wake up
so she could come with me.

I won't be angry with Gracie.

I hope Sarah isn't angry with me.

Will Sarah find my note?
Will she understand?
Will she understand
I couldn't take her with me
if I didn't know where I was going?

I want to go home,
but I can't go home.

Can I?

How can I go home?

How can I go home to Father?
What will he say?
What will he think?
Will he think I have not been good?

But I can't go back to the school,
where they think I am a thief.

I can't.

If my father hears
they think I am a thief,
he will forgive me for not being good
because even if I forget to march
when I should
and laugh with Gracie
when I should not
and speak Mohawk
when I should not
and run away
when I should not,
he knows I am not a thief.

But maybe he will not know
Mrs. Dwyer called me a thief.

So I must try to go home.

I thought if I followed
the tracks from the train
that brought us here,
I could find my way home.

I thought if I let the sun
shine on my right shoulder
through the hours of the morning,
I could find my way home.

I thought if I followed
the brightest star of Little Bear
through the darkness of the night,
I could find my way home.

But the wooden pieces
that held the iron rails in place
were too hard to walk on.
They slowed me down
when what I wanted most was
to be fast away from the school.
So I walked beside the tracks,
not on them, and in the dark,
I found they disappeared.

The clouds hid the stars
from my sight
and the morning rain
kept the sun asleep
and me hiding in an old barn,
where the smell of musty hay
made my stomach ache.

When the rain stopped
and I began again,
there was no sun or star to guide me.

So now I walk and walk in circles,
going nowhere.

saraн

"So, obviously, she did," Ida taunts
from across the table where we sit eating supper.

I lift my eyes from my plate, where the potatoes,
lying in flattened lumps, have turned cold.

I lift my eyes and tell her with my eyes
that she is wrong, that my sister is not a thief,
but when I open my mouth to tell her,
no sound comes out.

"Cat got your tongue?" Ida says, smirking,
waving her fork back and forth in the air.

I cannot help myself.

My hand shoots to my mouth,
and I turn to look for a cat.

And Ida laughs.

And my face grows warm.

Mattie, Mattie, Mattie.
Where have you gone?

mattie

The distant sound of a whistle
drifts through my head,
and as I open my eyes,
a stream of sun shines
through the cracks of the shed
and warms my face.

I bolt upright.
My heart begins to pound.

I heard it.
I know I heard it.

A whistle.
A train whistle.
A train.

My hands shake as I reach
for the sack beside me.
It holds what remains
of the little food that
Gracie and I collected
for what I thought would be
our journey together.

My fingers curl around
the coarse woolen threads
as I spring to my feet.

I move quickly toward
the wooden door, which,

missing one hinge,
hangs slightly open,
the morning light
urging me forward.

But before I reach the opening,
I stumble against a lump
that was not there
when I sought shelter from the rain
sometime in the darkness of last night.
As I fall backward into a corner,
my eyes adjust to the morning light
enough to see the lump shift and twist.

"Uunnnhh," the lump moans
as it begins to take shape,
moving upward
into a sitting position
with arms stretching above it.

I hear it again.

A whistle.
A train whistle.
A train.

I must follow the sound.

I must find the tracks.

I must follow the tracks.

I must find my home.

But between me and the train,
between me and home,
is a moaning lump that smells bad.

I sink into the wall behind me,
trying to make myself smaller,
trying to be quiet,
wondering if this lump
can hear my heart pounding wildly,
like the constant beating
of the drums for a dance,
and though I hold my breath,
my throat aches to cough.

"Uunnnhh," the lump moans again
as it slowly settles back down
onto the dirt floor.

A shiver begins at my feet
and moves upward.
At first I think it is the fear I feel,
but the dampness of my clothes
and the cold that has clung to me
for two nights is winning
the battle with my throat.

I press my fisted fingers
tightly against my mouth,
but I cannot stop the cough
that seems to echo endlessly
throughout the shed.

"Huh?" the lump moans
as it moves awkwardly

to an upright position
and turns to face me.

Two cloudy blue eyes
buried in a tangled mass of hair
exchange stares with my own.

"Whaddaya doin' here?"
a raspy voice asks.

I pull my bag close to my chest
to provide a shield
between me and this man
who has risen to his feet.

I open my mouth to speak
but only a cough
escapes into the air.

"Whaddaya got there?" he asks
as he moves toward me.

Thick hands caked with dirt
stretch forward.

"Ya got any food?"

I hear it again.

The whistle.

Louder. Closer.

"C'mon, give it here," he says,
grabbing the sack from my hands
as he shoves me to one side.

While he reaches into the sack
for the lone piece of bread,
the only one left
from the small store of food,
I bolt past him, heading
toward the doorway,
only to be stopped sharply
as he swings his arm
out in one quick move
and loops it around my throat,
pulling me up against him
so closely that between the
sour smell of his breath
and the tightness of his arm,
I cannot breathe.

"Not so fast. What else you got?"

Let me go.
Let me go, I scream in my head.

No sound and no air
comes out of my throat.

The train whistle sounds far away,
and the morning light starts to dim,
and my body begins to sink.

AKE'NISTENHA

Mother

I see my mother.

"No-o-o-o-o," I hear myself scream
as my lungs fill once more with air.

I hunch my shoulders forward
and shrink my body downward;
I slide beneath his arm
and sink to the dirt,
scrambling at once toward the door.

For the second time on my journey,
I am glad I am small.

"Git back here," he growls,
grabbing at my foot,
pulling me backward.

But as I claw the dirt,
the fingers of my left hand
feel the roughness
of a small stone,
and in one quick move,
I scoop it up and turn
to face my enemy,
flinging my only hope
smack into his face.

"Yeeoow," he yelps.
"You little bitch.
You little squaw bitch."

But I am already out of the shed,
running toward the morning light,
toward the sound of the distant train
that holds my hope of home.

sarah

"I miss her, too," Miss Weston whispers
as she squats low beside my desk,
where I stare at the primer opened flat before me.

I do not want to look at her.

I do not want to see if blue eyes
can be as sad as brown ones.

I hear the sadness in her voice,
but there is nothing to say.

There is nothing I want to say.

"Mattie is smart," she says, "and strong.
Don't worry. She will be safe."

She pats my arm gently, but I am angry,
angry because she is wrong
and she does not know she is wrong.

Mattie's spirit is strong,
but Mattie is not strong.

And if Miss Weston liked Mattie as much
as Mattie likes Miss Weston, then she would know,
she would know that my sister is not body strong.

"Do you know where she might be?" she asks,
closing the unread book on my desk,

waiting for me to look at her,
looking for my full attention.

But it is attention that I am not willing to give.

I have no answer.

Mattie's note that I wanted to keep,
Mattie's note that I put in the stove
because I did not dare even to hide it,
Mattie's note did not say she was going home.
Mattie's note was not a good-bye.
Mattie's note was a gift.

We will always be sisters.
The memory of my basket will live forever.
I give you that memory.

I shrug my shoulders and open the book
once more to a page that means nothing to me.

"She must have said something to you,"
she declares in a tone edged with annoyance,
a tone that says she has lost her patience with me.

"Please tell me, Sarah."

I say nothing.

She rises and I am glad,
glad that her eyes are above me,
that she cannot see into my thoughts.

Mattie would trust Miss Weston with her thoughts.

But I am not Mattie.

"She is probably trying to go home, isn't she?"

I shrug my shoulders once more.

I do not know where my sister is.

MATTIE

The morning sun
stayed long enough
for me to find the tracks
that could take me home,
but by the time
it should have been high overhead
it had disappeared once more
behind the darkening clouds,
and the rain returned.

I rested for eternity
under the scant shelter of a sumac,
waiting for the rain to stop.

But it didn't.

I watched the trains
as they thundered by,
some heading north
toward home
and some heading back
toward school.

I wondered when
and where they might stop
so that I might find a way
to board one heading north.

So many train cars passed by.
Many had windows like the one
that Sarah and I sat in,

peering out as we traveled
farther and farther
away from home.

So many people must be
on those many trains,
sitting side by side in their seats,
but through the rain
I could not see any faces
that peered out like mine and Sarah's.

So many train cars passed by,
many that were big boxes
with openings in their sides
that revealed nothing but darkness.

I begged for those empty boxes
filled with darkness
to stop and take me home.

But they didn't.

sarah

I cannot stop my legs from shaking as I stand before
the door that leads to where Mrs. Dwyer waits for me.

Miss Prentiss hurried into the classroom
while we were practicing our spelling
and said that Mrs. Dwyer wanted to see me.

Now.

All eyes fell on me as the room fell silent,
and I felt my cheeks grow warm.

I asked Miss Weston with my eyes,
without making a sound,
if I had to go, and she answered *yes*
with only a slight nod of her head.

I slid away from the safety of my desk
and walked slowly toward the door where
Miss Prentiss stood, stiff and scowling,
looking more and more like Mrs. Dwyer
with every step I took.

"Come, come. I haven't got all day,"
she said impatiently, tapping her foot—
tap, tap, tap—against the wooden floor
just like Mrs. Dwyer taps her ruler—
tap, tap, tap—into the palm of her hand.

And so across the yard we marched,
she in front and I behind,

like two soldiers heading into battle,
she eagerly and I lagging behind as much as I dared,
until she reached the steps where she stood,
tapping her foot—*tap, tap, tap*—against the stone,
waiting for me to catch up.

I found myself moving slower and slower,
wondering what I had done, why I was here,
and yet not wanting to know.

Mr. Davis, who stood at the corner of the building,
stopped his raking and lifted his head
to look at me just as I reached the bottom step.
Our eyes met briefly and I was sure I saw
his shoulders rise and fall as though he sighed.

Even Mr. Davis must have thought I was in trouble.

"Go ahead," Miss Prentiss commanded,
stepping aside for me to enter the end of the building,
where, on the first floor just inside to the right,
I would find Mrs. Dwyer waiting for me.

I have never been here before,
but I know this is where she lives.

Everyone knows.

So here I stand in the hall outside her door
with my arms and legs shaking so much
that I cannot control my hand enough
to lift it up and knock on the door.

"Come, come, now; she doesn't have all day,"

Miss Prentiss says as she swoops past me
and pounds loudly three times on the door
with her hand closed tightly into a fist
and then spins around and brushes past me,
escaping through the door to freedom.

The latch clicks, and the door before me swings open,
and Mrs. Dwyer appears, scowling down at me.

She steps to one side and motions for me to enter.

"Come in, Sarah, I want to talk to you."
Her voice shows no anger, but it is hard and cold.

I will not cry. I will not cry. I will not cry.

But my legs are shaking so much as I move
into the room that I fear my body will collapse
right here in Mrs. Dwyer's room,
and then what would I do?

Mattie would not cry.
Mattie would not collapse.

Mattie would stick out her chin
and stare back into Mrs. Dwyer's
black and beady eyes.

But I am not Mattie
and my eyes betray me and will not go
where I tell them to go, looking slightly down
at the pale white hand placed against a hip,
instead of upward into the face of the woman
who has made my sister leave me.

"I believe I have something of your sister's,"
she says as she closes the door behind me
and moves farther into the room.

"At least that is what I am told," she adds,
pausing with her back to me, facing a small table
next to the only window in the room.

Mattie's? She has something of Mattie's?
She has won my attention, and I lift my eyes.
She turns slowly and lifts her hands
as though she were proudly presenting an offering,
and what she offers catches me off my guard.

"Mattie's basket," I shout, surprised and relieved.

Instantly, Mrs. Dwyer pulls the basket back,
pressing it against her stomach,
protecting it with her hands as though I
were going to try to snatch it from her.

"So," she announces triumphantly, "it *is* hers."

And I realize I have made a grave mistake.
And I am angry. Angry at myself.
Angry at myself for being trapped.
Angry at myself for being afraid.

I am not going to cry.

I am too angry to cry.

"Please," I say, trying not to sound angry,
but fearing the firmness in my voice

gives me away. "Give it to me.
It is Mattie's basket . . . just her sewing basket."

"A sewing basket?" Mrs. Dwyer scoffs.
"There were no sewing supplies in this basket,
and a basket, a basket that should not be here at all,
a basket hidden away secretly in a bottom drawer
can be for no good."

Why does she have Mattie's basket?

How does she know where Mattie kept it?

Who is it who must hate Mattie so much
that she would steal her dearest possession
and give it to her harshest critic?

"Besides," she adds, "Matilda is no longer here.
Therefore, I guess she does not need her . . .
sewing basket, does she?"

And then she stretches her arms out forward,
holding Mattie's precious basket in the air,
as though she is offering it to me.

But as I lift my arms to take it from her,
she pushes her hands together in one sharp
movement, and Mattie's beautiful basket
made from our mother's love
is turned instantly into a misshapen mass
that now looks oddly like a small winter squash
flattened on one side from where it grew
pressed against a stone;
and without another word

Mrs. Dwyer takes two steps to her right
and drops the object of her scorn
into the waste bin that sits beside a wooden chair
placed against the wall; and as I hear it hitting
the empty bottom with a dull thud,
the emptiness inside me presses against my heart.

But I do not cry.

I am too angry to cry.

"You had no right to do that," I shout,
surprised that the sound of my voice
and the choice of my words
sound so much like Mattie.

"I want my sister's basket," I demand.

But she ignores me, and even my anger
cannot overcome my fear
and force me to step forward
to retrieve what she so lightly cast aside.

"You may go now, Sarah," she says,
dismissing me with a wave of her hand.

I cannot move.

"Now, Sarah!" she commands.

I turn and leave, empty-handed,
angry and ashamed,
angry at myself for being so afraid,

ashamed of myself for being so afraid.

But I will not cry.

I am too angry to cry.

MATTIE

The sky has stopped the rain
but the warmth of the sun,
which has once more appeared,
cannot stop my body from shaking
as I kneel on the ground,
hidden behind a stalk,
pulling back the husk
from an ear of corn.

At home,
we would have long ago
gathered the Three Sisters,
the squash and corn and beans,
that grow in the field
between our barn
and the great river,
and what had not been gathered
would have softened from the frost.

If I must be so far from home,
I am grateful that the frost
has not yet arrived
and that the farmer's field
beside the endless tracks
still holds something
to ease my hunger.

The corn is hard and dry,
but I was so hungry
it was easy to pretend

that it is just as tender and sweet
as the corn that Father grows.

My stomach says I am full,
but many kernels are left on the cob,
so I press the husk back in place.

I gather three more ears.

If I had not lost my bag
to the man in the shed,
I would take more,
but the ears of corn
are long and thick
and too hard to carry
with my arms shaking so.

It's good that I don't need to eat much.

I think of my mother
roasting corn over hot coals
in the chill of an autumn evening
as we all hovered near,
waiting eagerly.
For just a moment,
the memory of warm husks
held in our hands
takes away the cold I feel.

But as I press the ears
tightly to my chest
to keep them from sliding away,
the wetness of my dress

sets me shivering once more.

I think I shall never
be warm again.

sараH

"What did she want?" Gracie whispers,
sitting down beside me on the bed,
folding her hands neatly in her lap.

I shrug my shoulders in response.

"Are you in trouble?" she persists.

Everyone, everyone in the whole school,
must know that I was sent to see Mrs. Dwyer.

I shake my head from side to side.
I do not want to talk.
I do not want to talk to anyone,
except Mattie.

"I am sorry," she says.

Her words catch me by surprise.
I wonder why she would say she is sorry.

Is she sorry for me?

Is she sorry for Mattie?

Is she sorry that she is not the one in trouble?

"I should have gone with her," she adds,
and I am surprised that I find comfort in her words.

I am glad she did not say empty words to me,

that Mattie is brave and that Mattie is strong,
that Mattie will be all right.

"**Ontiatshi ne'e**," she says loudly, not caring
who hears her speak in the language of the people.

She did not need to tell me that Mattie is her friend.

She puts her arm around my shoulder,
and I am surprised that I find comfort in her touch.

"**Nia:wen**," I say quietly to Mattie's friend,
Mattie's friend who has become mine.

MATTIE

"You there. Girl! You there."

Fear.

I do not dare to turn
toward the voice
though I know
it is me he calls for.

"Hey, you there."

Escape?

The tracks across the field
seem so far away.

I try to run
but the ears of corn
in my shaking arms
and the wetness of my skirt
around my weary legs
slow me into a dreamlike movement
where, no matter how hard I try,
my body will not move,
cannot move, fast enough.

I let the ears of corn drop
to the ground beside me
and swing my arms,
back and forth, back and forth,
to move me forward,

but just as my legs respond,
a hand clamps onto my shoulder
and its heaviness forces me
down into a heap
onto the muddy ground.

"Hey there, girl. You all right?"

The voice sounds surprised,
and as I look up at the face
staring into my own,
there is surprise in his eyes as well.

He reaches down
and slips his hand, gently,
under my elbow
and lifts me to my feet.

"C'mon, you come with me," he says.
"Let's get you up to the house."

My head tells me
I should look for an escape,
but my body tells me I cannot.

A firmness in his voice
tells me not to run,
but the softness of his tone
tells me not to be afraid.

He turns me toward
the gray buildings
clustered together
at the end of the field;

side by side,
we walk slowly
over the clumps of mud
and through the tangled mass
of dying plants.

My heart pounds
faster and faster
at each step I take,
but I am too tired
and too cold to care.

When we reach the porch,
he pushes me forward,
up the steps and through a door
into the warmest room
I have ever been in,
at least since I left home.

Warmth.

"Look here, Agnes," the man says
in a jovial, booming voice.
"Look what I found in the field."

Agnes is the woman at the stove,
her enormous back facing us,
her right elbow moving in circles,
and though her immense body,
almost as wide as the stove,
blocks my view and
keeps me from seeing
what holds her attention,

I suspect she stirs something
cooking on the stove.

The thought of something,
anything, anything
warm inside me
evaporates any fear I hold.

"And just what did you—"
she begins as she turns,
stopping short when her eyes,
full of surprise, fall on me.

"Well, my goodness, Hiram,
what have we here!"
she exclaims, turning slightly
to drop the spoon back into the pot.

"Found her in the field, stealing corn."

Yes, now I am a thief.

"Well, she looks half-starved.
Come here, child, sit down, sit down."

Kindness.

She pulls a wooden chair
away from the table
and motions for me to sit,
and when I see her reaching
for a bowl on the shelf,
I move to the table slowly,
but willingly.

As I settle into the chair,
a bowl of steaming soup
is placed before me.

"Come, come," she says, "you eat. Now.
No one around me needs to be hungry.
No one around me needs to steal food.
Ain't that the truth, Hiram?"

"That's the truth, Agnes."

She thinks I am hungry.

I am not hungry.

I am cold.

I dip the spoon into the broth,
ever so slowly so that the shaking
of my hand is not noticed,
and lift it to my lips.

The smell of the soup is rich with herbs
and the steam warms my face,
and my body begins to relax.

"You got a name, child?"

I stare into my soup.

"You from the Indian school, ain't you?"
she continues in a voice
that is not unkind.

I stare into my soup.

"Sure she's from that school,"
he says. "Jus' look at her.
Bet she don't speak English yet."

I stare into my soup.

"She can't be on an Outing,"
Agnes says quietly.

"We would know if she was workin'
for anyone 'round here," she adds,
"wouldn't we?"

Why have they softened their voices
if they think I do not understand
what they say?

"Hard to tell," the man says, "maybe she's
new and just got lost doin' an errand."

"Stealing corn?" Agnes responds.

Hiram starts to pace
back and forth, back and forth,
by the door.

"She's a runaway, ain't she, Hiram?"

Fear.

I sip the soup slowly from the spoon,
trying to keep my hand from shaking.

Hiram paces back and forth,
back and forth.

Agnes is quiet.

Suddenly I cannot keep the cold
inside me from coming out,
and I drop the spoon into the dish,
throwing my hands up
to cover my face
just as a sneeze explodes.

"My goodness," Agnes shouts,
"this child is wet clean through.
She needs to get outta those clothes."

I pick up the spoon once more,
pretending to eat as I watch Agnes.
Her enormous body waddles
through the doorway
into another room
and disappears from my view.

"Hiram," she calls loudly, "come here."

"Whadda you want?" he asks,
trudging into the next room.

"I need that box offa the top shelf,"
she hollers.

I rest the spoon quietly
on the edge of the dish
and slide my legs out

from under the table,
careful not to move the chair,
and again I am glad
that I am small.

"I need those clothes up there,"
she says. "Way up on top.
The ones I was givin' to the church."

I hear some shuffling movement.

"Bound to be somethin'
in that box she can wear."

I am almost to the door
when a loud clatter,
followed by a thump,
comes from the other room.

"Hiram," she exclaims,
"careful with that!"

He responds loudly
but I no longer
can hear the words
as I close the door
quietly behind me
and tell my legs
to run,
to run,
to run.

Freedom.

saraн

The rain beats against the window,
and when I close my eyes
I can picture Mattie and me
and our mother and father
and sisters and brothers
listening to the rain on the roof
as we sit around the table in our kitchen,
glad that the rain has come to nourish the earth.

But when I open my eyes because I cannot sleep,
and in the darkness see bed after bed,
in two long rows along the walls,
the image of home fades quickly,
and the empty bed I know is here reminds me
that Mattie is somewhere between here and home,
and I wonder if she, too, is somewhere
where she hears the same rain.

MATTIE

I sit on the bank of the creek,
hidden in the brush
behind the trunk of the willow,
the weeping tree whose branches
bend and sway with the wind,
and I listen to the train
whose whistle echoes softly
in the distance.

I try not to breathe
so I can listen.

I try not to cough
so I can listen,
waiting to hear
if the whistle blows again,
blows louder and so closer.

It is.

It is louder.

It is closer.

The rain has stopped,
and the morning sun
tells me the train
must be headed north.

Through leafless branches,
I stare at the tall tower

that stands on guard
on the other side of the tracks.

Waiting and hoping.

When Sarah and I
came to school on the train,
it stopped over and over again
by a tower as tall as this one,
a giant wooden bucket
on giant wooden legs.

I hope that the train
will stop here.

The wetness of my clothes
creates a chill I cannot shake
as I crouch behind
a mass of tangled branches.
I cough and cough,
holding my hands to my mouth,
muffling the sounds
that might travel on the wind.

I want to feel the warmth
of the sun.

I want to step away
from the dark shadows
and into the pool
of spreading sunshine.

But a man stands on a platform
near the tower,

pacing back and forth,
looking down the track.

I must wait for the train.

The train must be moving slowly.
I have heard the whistle blowing
for what seems like forever,
but I see nothing.

I wait and wait and wait.

And then, there it is, big and black,
moving toward me,
moving slowly, which is good
because if it is moving slowly
then maybe it will stop
beside the wooden tower.

And if it stops,
I can climb aboard
and soon I will be home.

The whistle blows
louder and louder,
and the train moves
slower and slower.

Yes, it will stop.

It will stop.

The whistle gives one long wail
and the wheels screech to a stop.

I escape from my hiding place,
scrambling from underneath
the tangle of branches,
standing up to quickly make my plan.

The sight of the long row of boxes
as far to the south as I can see
starts my heart pounding.

I cannot move.

I cannot breathe.

There is no hope.

Where are the empty boxes?
Where are the train's cars
with the big openings?

An endless, endless row of boxes,
all with solid walls.

Think, Mattie! Think!

A clang from the train
startles me into decision.

My hope must be on the other side.

I climb quickly up the steep bank
to the edge of the tracks,
take a deep breath
and drop to my knees,
crawling on hands and toes

under the train,
pausing only for a moment
at the other side to look
for signs of human movement
before I slide out cautiously
from underneath this mass of metal.

I spring upright and turn around
to face the train, looking quickly
to right and left.

Yes!

There are boxes to my right
with openings large enough
for me and all my family
to climb through at once.

But it is only me.

I run past one, two, three cars,
finally coming to an opening.

I stop sharply,
my hopes falling fast,
suddenly sadly aware
that my escape is halted,
not by a weakness of mind or will,
but only because I am too small.

I am too small.

There is no way for me
to climb onto the train.

If I stretch my arms,
I can reach the edge,
but even if I was not cold,
even if I was not tired,
I could not pull myself up
into the emptiness.

I look around,
desperate for some help.

A rock, a log, anything.

I do not see the man
who paced on the platform,
waiting, like me, for the train,
but I do see a small shed
just behind the tower,
and I know if there is any hope
it must be there.

I run down the bank
and hurry toward the shed,
using the sparse cover
of the bushes as my shield,
hoping the man who stood
waiting on the platform is busy,
hoping the train will not soon leave.

I hear voices, muffled sounds,
as I sneak up behind the shed.
I cannot hear the words they say,
so I am certain they must be closer
to the train than they are to me.

Behind the wooden shed
lies a metal bucket,
missing the handle
and bashed in on one corner.

I hope it can make me tall enough
to reach the edge of the empty car.

With my salvation in my arms,
I hurry back through the bushes,
but the sound of the train's whistle
and the grinding of metal against metal
warns me the train is soon to leave
and all caution is thrown aside
as I break into the open,
running faster and faster,
faster than tired legs can go.

"Hey, there," a voice behind me bellows.
"Hey, there. Whadda you up to?"

My heart is pounding
as I reach the opening
and slam the bucket upside down
into the stones beside the track.
I step up onto its bottom,
my elbows planted onto the rim
of the opening's wooden edge,
and lean into the darkness.

"You there," the voice hollers.
"Git away from there afore you git hurt."

I hear footsteps
crunching on the stones,
and as I look quickly to my left,
I see the man from the platform
running toward me.

"Git down," he yells. "Git down."

"No," I shout, pressing my arms
onto the wooden floor
as the train rumbles and groans
and jumps into motion.

"I'm going home."

But it is too late.

The whistle blows once more,
and the car heaves itself forward.

The bucket beneath me tips over
and my arms, weak and tired,
cannot hold me up any longer,
and my body, wet and shivering,
tumbles onto the moving ground.

My hopes are gone.

saraн

"Sarah," someone whispers at my side,
and as I turn toward the voice,
a pile of clean clothes, that I must sort and fold,
is placed in a heap on the table before me.

It is Ruthie.

"She is back," she whispers,
her unsmiling eyes staring straight ahead,
her hands fussing unnecessarily
with the clean clothes on the table.

"They found her," she explains as though I might
have thought my sister had chosen to return to school.

My chin drops and my mouth falls open
as though I am about to say something.

But I have nothing to say.

I would have told Mattie not to run away.

I would have told her to stay,
stay with me, stay here at the school,
stay so she could tell everyone that Mrs. Dwyer
made a mistake, that Mrs. Dwyer was wrong,
that she, Mattie Tarbell, is no thief.

But Mattie did not ask me.

She ran away in the night.

She left a note beside me while I slept,
a note that did not tell me where she was going
though I knew she must be going home
because where else could Mattie go?

And Gracie would not answer me
when I asked her if she knew that Mattie had gone,
when I asked her if she knew where Mattie had gone.

Gracie hid her face in her hands and cried.

But I did not cry.

Mattie was gone and I was still here
and I knew she would tell me I was not to cry,
that I had to be good for both of us now.

So for three days I have cried inside myself.

But no one,
not Ruthie,
not Gracie,
not Miss Weston,
not Mr. Davis,
not Miss Prentiss,
not Mrs. Dwyer,
no one will ever see me cry.

"How do you know?" I whisper to Ruthie
when I find my voice again.

She does not speak,
but as she slowly turns toward another table,
carrying the folded stack of clean clothes,

she answers my question with a slight nod of her head
toward Ida, who stands near the door,
her head stretched forward,
looking out into the yard.

My heart sinks to my stomach as Ida turns toward me
and answers my stare with a smile that says she knows and is glad,
and I worry that Mattie is in more trouble.

MATTIE

"If you tell me where it is,"
she says without looking at me,
pacing back and forth,
back and forth,
tapping her ruler
into the palm of her hand,
"it will be easier on you."

My eyes follow her,
back and forth,
back and forth.

My head hurts
and my legs are tired
and my voice won't work
because I have no answer.

"You will be punished,"
she continues,
"but your punishment
can be one that reflects
the mercy of those of us
who only want what is best
for you and for the school."

She stops pacing
and turns to face me,
but when our eyes meet,
I cannot hold my head up
any longer and so I search
the wooden floor for help.

Where is the answer
she wants to hear?

"But, Matilda," she snaps,
"if you do not return my brooch
and show remorse for your behavior,
if you persist in this stubbornness,
then mercy cannot be an option."

I would give her an answer
if I had one.

I am tired and cold.
My clothes have dried on the outside,
but they are wet yet close to my skin,
and there is a dampness that sends
shivers throughout my body.

And she wants her pin.

"I want to see my sister," I whisper.

The sound of my own voice startles me.

"What?" she bellows at me,
her voice shattering the air so loudly
my already aching head
begins to throb.

I don't want to see Sarah.

I don't want Sarah to see me.

I don't want Sarah to be in trouble.

"I want to see my sister," I say again
before I can stop the words.

"You are impossible," she says,
but her voice is quiet,
quieter perhaps
than I have ever heard her voice.

"I was prepared to be lenient,"
she continues. "I was prepared
to let you mend your stubborn ways,
but you are impossible. . . ."

She is suddenly so quiet
that I want to lift my head
to see what she is doing,
but my head is tired.

No one is moving.

No one is saying anything.

Not Mrs. Dwyer.
Not the man who stands beside her.
Not the two men who stand behind me,
the two men who talked for a long time
with the man who works at the tower,
the two men who brought me
back to the school, back to Mrs. Dwyer,
the two men who were not unkind,
but who said nothing
to me as we returned,
nor I to them.

In the silence it seems
like hours have passed
and when she speaks again
it is as though she is waking me
from a deep sleep.

"Well, Matilda,"
she says slowly and calmly,
but with an iciness that sends a chill
throughout my whole body,
which is already shivering with cold.

"I am prepared to give you time,
some time alone,
where you can think
about being more cooperative
before we take more drastic measures."

She pauses.

I hear her dress rustling,
as though she has turned to move,
but I hear no steps on the wooden floor.

"Does that seem fair to you, Mr. Remsen?"

I have never seen Mr. Remsen,
but I know who he is.

Gracie said she heard
we weren't ever in real trouble
unless we were sent to see Mr. Remsen.

Miss Weston sent two of the older boys

to see Mr. Remsen when they got in a fight
in the classroom and broke a window.

Miss Prentiss once asked Mrs. Dwyer,
while they were inspecting our rooms,
if she should send for Mr. Remsen,
but Mrs. Dwyer said no,
that she could handle it . . .
whatever *it* was.

But I had never seen Mr. Remsen.

"More than fair, Mrs. Dwyer,"
the man beside her answers.

saraн

With every step I take
on the pebbles along the path,
I hear a noise louder than the thunder of rain
on the roof of my grandmother's home.

I hold my breath
for fear that someone will hear me,
for fear I will be stopped,
and so I move from the path onto the grass
and continue past the bandstand and across the yard,
darting through the single shaft of moonlight
spread between the schoolhouse and the large oak.

I step cautiously into the shadows
near the stone guardhouse
where my sister must sleep now.

If I should be seen,
I, too, will be sleeping
in the guardhouse
with Mattie.

I reach deeply into the pocket of my dress
to feel the bread and the apple
I took from the dining hall for Mattie,
and I wonder if stealing an apple and bread
will put me in the guardhouse.

"Mattie," I call quietly
toward the barred window
which sits high above my head.

Silence.

"Mattie," I repeat. "It's me."

There is no answer.

I wonder if Mattie is asleep.

Maybe she has died in that dark place
and left me all alone.

Mattie would not do that, would she?

"Mattie," I call again, louder.

It will not matter if someone hears me
if Mattie is dead.

"Sarah?" I hear her question softly.

"It's me, Mattie. I brought you some food."

"Go away, Sarah," she whispers sharply.
"Someone will see you."

"I brought you some food," I repeat.
"Are you hungry? Did they feed you?"

I think I hear her crying, but she does not answer.
I think she does not want to tell me that she is hungry.
I think she does not want me to hear her crying.

Suddenly, a large figure
steps out of the darkness from around the corner

of this stone building that holds my sister,
and my heart and stomach become one.

I turn to run,
but my legs barely reach the moonlight
when I feel a strong grip on my shoulder,
and as a cry works its way out of my throat,
a hand presses softly against my mouth.

"Shh," a voice whispers in my ear.

My heart pounds wildly,
and I twist my body to escape,
but when I see it is Mr. Davis,
dear Mr. Davis who has pulled me
into the shadows out of the moonlight,
my fear evaporates into the dark.

As our eyes meet,
he lifts his hand from my mouth
and puts one finger to his lips.

"Oh, Mr. Davis," I whisper.

Mr. Davis will not tell on me.
Mr. Davis is my friend.

"What you up to, missy?"
he asks as he crouches down beside me,
his black face barely visible
against the blackness of the stone wall.

"I have something for my sister," I tell him,
holding my pocket open as proof,

though I know in the dark
he cannot see what it is I have.

"Some food," I explain.

"Well, den, well, den," he says softly,
"we mus' see dat she gets it."

And so I know I am right.
Mr. Davis is a friend and I am grateful.

"Nia:wenkowa," comes out of my mouth
before I can stop it, and I do not care.

Mr. Davis is my friend.
He will not tell on me.

"Thank you, thank you."

"Come now," he whispers, "we mus' be quiet
or we all be in trouble."

"Mattie has to get out," I tell him.
"Can you help me get my sister out?"

Even in the dark, I see his head
move from side to side,
and my heart sinks.

"No, missy. No one gets outta dis place,"
he explains as he turns his face toward the wall
and presses the palm of his hand against the stone,
"not until dey decide she been punished enough,
not until dey sure dat she ain't gonna run away."

I press my hand against the stone, too.
It is hard and cold.

"But Mattie will die if she stays here," I tell him.

"No, no. Yo' sister aint gonna die," he whispers
as he rises, lifting me slowly upward
with his strong hands pressed against my sides
until the window is within my reach.

"She got you."

MATTIE

My ear presses against the stone,
but the wall which separates me
from my sister is thick.

I can hear voices.
I cannot hear what they say,
but she cannot be alone.

"Mattie?"

It is Sarah's voice I hear.

"Mattie? Here.
Something for you.
Please take it."

Through the darkness
I see her arm stretch through the bars,
and my heart begins to pound.
Sarah is taller than I am, but she
could not reach the window on her own,
and so I know she cannot be alone.

"Mattie," her voice demands.
"Say something."

"Who is with you?" I ask.

"Mr. Davis. It is all right.
He will not tell," she tells me.
"He can help you."

No one can help me now.

"No, Sarah, go back to your room.
I will be back with you soon."

In the darkness,
I see the outline of her arm
as it swings back and forth.

"Can you reach this?" she asks.

"Almost," I tell her. "Hold still."

I step up on the edges of my toes,
my left hand pressed against the wall
to keep from falling forward,
and stretch my right hand upward,
and as I wrap my fingers around
the roundness of an apple, our fingers
touch slightly just before I fall back
onto the flatness of my feet.

"NIA:WENKOWA."

I am grateful for my sister,
grateful she has Mr. Davis.

But I cannot have Sarah in trouble.

"Go back to the dormitory," I demand
in the strongest voice I can manage
in a whisper. "Go. Now."

"Here," she says. "Take this, too."

Her arm dangles again through the bars,
and once more I stretch upward to take
her offering, bread, bread I do not want.

There is an emptiness inside me.

I do not know
if I am hungry or not,
but it does not matter
because there is nothing
that could fill the emptiness
inside me.

"Now, go," I insist.

"Come, we bes' be gone now,"
I hear the deep voice of Mr. Davis say.

"I'll be back, Mattie," she insists.
"Tomorrow night."

"No," I tell her sharply,
almost forgetting to whisper.
"You stay away, Sarah Tarbell.
Stay away. You hear me?"

I can hear their voices,
but they are quiet,
distant once more,
and I know that Mr. Davis
has lowered her to the ground.

"Mr. Davis," I call quietly,
"you must tell her, tell her

she is not to come back."

There is no answer
and I wonder if he has heard me.

saraH

Miss Weston does not see that I stand here,
waiting for her to see me waiting for her
to finish what she is writing.

She is my only hope.

She likes Mattie.

If I wait here much longer,
I will be in trouble with Mrs. Hunter,
grumpy old Mrs. Hunter, who works now
in the laundry watching us the way Miss Velma did,
only Miss Velma did not scowl the way Mrs. Hunter does.

"Oh my, Sarah," Miss Weston says,
finally looking up. "You startled me."

"I am sorry, Miss Weston," I say.

"What is it, dear?"

The softness of her voice
and the kindness of her words startle me.

Miss Weston called me "dear."

"Is there something you need, Sarah?"
she continues when I do not answer.

"Mattie needs your help, Miss Weston," I blurt out.
"Can you help her?"

She turns her eyes away from me quickly
and looks down at the papers on her desk,
and my heart sinks into the soles of my feet.

"I don't know," she says, tapping her fingers on the desk,
her eyes still looking at her papers.

Miss Weston was my only hope.

"If you cannot help," I say, turning away slowly,
forcing my feet toward the door,
"then she is lost."

Mattie

The door creaks open
and the light from outside
filters quickly into the dark room
where I sit on the stone floor.

The shadow of a woman
appears in the opening,
but my eyes are tired,
and I cannot see who it is.

I wonder if Mrs. Dwyer
thinks I will tell her
what she thinks I can tell her,
which I can't.

"Mattie?"

I know that voice instantly,
and my heart starts to pound.

"Miss Weston?" I ask quietly,
for fear my ears
may have falsely heard,
giving me hope
when I feared there was none.

"Come, child," she says.

saraн

I look out the window and cannot believe my eyes.
It is Mattie and Miss Weston walking down the path.

I drop the dress into the sink and rush to the door.

"Sarah," Mrs. Hunter shouts out sharply.
"Just where do you think you are going?"

"It is my sister," I tell her, my hand on the knob
that I have not yet turned.

"I must see my sister."

The other girls stop what they are doing,
and their eyes move from me to Mrs. Hunter
and back to me.

Ruthie runs toward the window.

"Ruthie," Mrs. Hunter yells harshly.

Ruthie stops and slowly returns to the table
where garments piled high wait for her attention.

"Please," I ask. "Please, Mrs. Hunter."

Mrs. Hunter comes toward me,
and I hold my breath.
She is not as nice as Miss Velma was,
and her face only knows how to frown,
but she has never been mean.

She stops at the window nearest to the door
and peers out, her hand arched above her brow
to shield the sun, which once again shines brightly.

"Hmm," she says softly to herself, her iron-gray hair
leaning more and more toward the window,
her eyes squinting as she follows the movement
that I cannot see through the wooden door
that separates me from my sister.

"Hard to tell," she says, but not to me.
"Looks like they are headed toward the infirmary."

"Oh, no," I blurt out. "Mattie must be sick."

I pull open the door, but Mrs. Hunter's arm
reaches out and slams it shut.

"Miss Weston is with her," she says firmly.
"She will see that she is taken care of."

"But she's my sister," I plead.

"That may be," Mrs. Hunter adds.
"But there's nothing you can do.
The best way to help her is to be a good girl
and go back to work."

"But—"

"Now!"

MATTIE

"I'm fine,"
I lie to Sarah and the others
as Sarah and I sit side by side
on her bed while the other girls
hover around us.

Ruthie sits on her own bed
facing us,
smiling more
than I have ever seen her smile,
smiling more at Sarah
than at me,
happy, I hope,
for Sarah, not for me.

Gracie is nowhere to be seen.
Her absence hurts my heart.

I wonder if she is happy
that I am back.

There is no happiness
in my return.
Not for me.

I wonder how many
of the many eyes that stare,
that stare at me sitting here,
with Sarah's arm wrapped

warmly around me,
still think I am a thief.

And now I am a failure.

"I'm fine," I say again.
"The nurse told Miss Weston to
see that I put on some dry clothes
and to make sure I eat."

That is not a lie. She did.

That's all she did.

When the nurse asked if I felt ill,
I told her no. I said I was just cold,
and she told Miss Weston
that I would be fine
once I had on some fresh clothes.

Miss Weston walked with me
across the yard to the dorm,
muttering all the way,
but I could not hear
what she said to herself.

I wanted to ask her many things:
Why did they let me out?
Had Mrs. Dwyer's brooch been found?
What will happen to me now?

But I only asked her one thing:
Would she be in trouble for helping me?

I wondered if she would be sent away
like Miss Velma.

She did not answer me.

She just kept muttering to herself,
her voice soft but words flying quickly,
and the only words I understood were
"should never have been"
and I did not know what she meant.

I only know that my heart says
I should never have been found.

"Mattie," Sarah whispers to me,
"I'm glad you are safe."

The voices around me
now begin to buzz,
all speaking at once,
all filled with curiosity.

"Where were you?"

"Were you hungry?"

"Were you scared?"

"How did they find you?"

"How far did you get?"

I lean against Sarah's body,
feeling her warmth.

I know she will not be hurt
by my words.

"Not far enough," I answer.

saraн

"Mattie," I urge quietly from the edge of my bed,
where I sit tying my shoes that suddenly seem
too small, and I wonder if I might ask for another pair.

Now that I am a woman, I seem to be growing so fast.

"Mattie, you get up now."

She rolls over, and the blanket that covered
her head now falls away from her face.

"I'm sick," she moans.

I cannot see her eyes in the darkness of the room.
Mattie's eyes tell me the truth; they tell the truth
even when the truth is nowhere to be seen by others,
so if I could see her eyes I would know,
but it is too dark.

"You stop pretending, Mattie. Stop pretending
and get up," I urge once more.

I will not believe that my sister is sick.

The springs of my bed creak as I stand up slowly,
planting my feet firmly on the wooden floor,
feeling the pinch of my toes as they push
against the inside ends of my shoes.

"I don't feel good," she says.

"You will be in trouble again," I whisper loudly
as I move around the ends of the two beds
that separate me from my sister.

"I don't care," she mutters as she rolls over
and faces the wall.

I will not believe that my sister is sick.

Mattie can be so stubborn,
and if she does not get up now,
she will pay for her stubbornness once more,
and I cannot bear the thought of Mattie
being locked away again.

"Mattie, please, get up *now*," I plead as I
sit down on the edge of the mattress.

She does not move.

"Mattie?"

I hear the quiet panic in my voice.
Where is her defiance now?
Where is her stubbornness?

"Mattie?"

I reach out and touch her lightly on the shoulder,
and her body moves up and down heavily.

"What's wrong?" Gracie asks softly
as she leans over my shoulder.
"Is she really sick?"

"I think so," I tell her, but I am not sure.
Mattie has often pretended to be sick,
or so I thought.

"Mrs. Dwyer will be angry," Gracie says
as she sits down on the edge of her bed.
In the increasing lightness of the early dawn,
I see her leaning forward,
her elbows pressing into her knees,
her chin settling into the palms of her hands.

"Mattie will be in trouble again." She sighs.
"What shall we do?"

I shake Mattie's shoulder.

"SATKETSKO," I demand. "Wake up!"

mattie

Sarah thought I pretended
to be sick today.
She has often thought
I pretended to be ill.
I have only pretended
to pretend.

"Mattie," she hissed at me.
"Mattie, you get up now."

"I'm sick," I explained.

I could feel the skin
on my forehead wrinkle
as I tried to open my eyes,
but the lids were too heavy
and I could not force them upward.

"You stop pretending.
You get up now," she scolded again
as the springs of her bed creaked.

"I don't feel good," I told her.

"You will be in trouble again,"
she whispered harshly.

"I don't care," I muttered
as I rolled over,
shivering with cold,
a tightness in my chest

sending sharp pains
throughout my body,
making it hard for me to breathe.

"Mattie, please, get up *now*."

I heard the fear in her voice,
and I knew she was right.

I would be in trouble.

Again.

Mrs. Dwyer would seize the chance
to scold and punish,
to scorn and criticize.

"You mind your step," she said to me
after I was released from the guardhouse,
where I was certain
I was destined to die.

"This matter is not over, yet," she said.
"I will watch your every move."

Sarah was right.

I would be in trouble.

I did not care.
I could not lift my head
from the pillow
that gave it no comfort.

"Mattie?"

Sarah's voice was so quiet,
I thought I heard it only in my mind.
I thought she might have left the room,
left me alone, until I felt her hand
pressing against my shoulder.

And then I heard Gracie,
and I knew that Gracie
was still my friend
and did not want me in trouble.

Again.

"SATKETSKO," I heard Sarah say.

A life of childhood
flashed through my head.
I heard my mother calling me
to rise for the day.

SATKETSKO, *Mattie. Come, now,*
time to start the day.

AKE'NISTENHA

Mother

With the gentle sounds
of my mother's voice urging me
to greet the morning,
I found my body moving
out of my bed.

Once more, I began pretending
that I had been pretending to be sick,
while Sarah chided me for scaring her so
and Gracie breathed deeply and sighed
as together they hurriedly helped me
into my clothes so I would not
be in trouble.

Again.

Yet, throughout the day
that passed as slowly
as the days of summer
when we were young,
I found Sarah staring at me,
in motherly fashion.

I know she must have known the truth.

saraн

Mattie and Gracie march, one behind the other,
off to lessons, but there is no laughter in their footsteps.

Mattie's laughter is gone.

This morning, I stomped in place beside my bed,
hoping Mattie would laugh, but she did not even smile.

Instead, she looked at me with sad eyes
and shook her head and said,
"You be good, Sarah."

Mattie is always good now.

If that is being good,
I do not want to be good ever again.

mattie

I sit at the machine, my foot
pressing up and down
awkwardly on the pedal,
pushing the material
under the needle
that bobs up and down
and catches the thread.

I don't remember the pedal
being so heavy.

"You are very fortunate,"
Miss Prentiss says,
standing beside me.

"Mrs. Dwyer is still very upset
with you, and she might have assigned
you elsewhere," she explains,
nodding as though the sewing room
would be everyone's choice,
if we had one.

She places a pile of clothing
on the table beside me.

"These need to be done
by the end of tomorrow.
Most should be done by hand,"
she says, and I wonder
if the pile has been waiting
for me to return.

I do not answer.

"Tomorrow, Mattie.
Did you hear me?"

I do not think about tomorrows,
not anymore.

I can only think about today.

"Mattie!" she says sharply.

"Yes, ma'am."

saraн

They should have sent her home.

They should have sent her home to Father.

They should have let her rest where she could hear
the river of our childhood beating against the shore,
perfect rhythm for her heart, which beats no longer.

They should have sent her home.

She called out to me in the night,
unaware I had crawled into the bed beside her.

We lay there together,
her body shaking with cold,
her nightgown drenched with sweat,
my body shaking with fear,
my gown wet from hers.

I wrapped my arms around her body,
which had grown smaller and smaller
since we had left home.

I wrapped my arms around her body,
holding her so close our hearts could have been one
if hers had not been beating harder and faster than my own,
if hers had not been crying out for peace
while mine cried out in fear.

And when morning came, and I awoke from the sleep
that we both had finally found, my arms were still

wrapped around her body,
but I was alone.

They should have sent her home.

They should have sent her home to Father.

Ida said Father must pay to have Mattie at home
and that we must be very poor if our father cannot.

She said she heard Mrs. Dwyer being angry with Miss Weston;
she said she heard her say that a telegram had been sent,
that Mattie's father knew, and that the matter was closed
and that it was not Miss Weston's business,
and so I had better not say anything to Mrs. Dwyer
because she was very, very upset with me
because I did not tell her that Mattie was sick.

They should have sent her home.

They should have sent her home to Father.

They should have sent her home so Father's farewell
was not the memory of a train clanging as it left the station.

Does Father know when Mattie's breath stopped?
Will Father know when ten days have passed so the feast can begin?

When my mother died, the message was told,
the GAI'WIIO', the good word of the Creator,
that we should put our grief aside when we have had
our one last look at our mother, and that when the feast
begins her soul will return to partake of it with us.

And so we took our last look, and she was buried near the river,
near her own mother, whose soul had left us not so long before,
and then the days went by and we had the feast
and our mother's soul was there
and the many gifts were given
to those who came and helped when her body died.

How will Father leave his grief behind
if he cannot take his one last look?

How will he know Mattie's soul is free if there is no feast?

They should have sent her home to Father.

They should have sent her home.

MATTIE

They should have sent me home.

I wish I could say it does not matter.

But it does.

I wish I could tell Sarah
that it does not matter.

But it does.

My body lies in unfamiliar ground,
with other children I never knew,
tucked away behind a building
far away from the grassy knoll
that feels the softness of the wind
that comes across our river,
which is where I would rest
if they had sent me home.

My spirit knows it does not matter.

It is no longer separated
from my mother
and her mother
and her mother.

But I remember well
how comforting it was
to walk over the earth where they lay,
how not long before we left

for our long journey on the train,
I had sat on the grass above my mother
and felt comforted by her memories,
not mourning, not grieving,
only remembering.

Above me now,
Sarah stretches out on the ground
the palms of her hands
blending into the earth
where no grass yet grows,
searching for comfort.

But she will not grow old in school.

Who will sit above me
when she has grown and gone?
Where will she find her comfort
when she is old?
I hope she will grow old
at home near our river,
a river so wide that the waves
flow in and out against the shore
and soothe us in our sleep,
even in our endless sleep.

I hope she will grow old.

I called out to her in the night,
and soon I knew she was beside me,
her body so hot and shaking so much
I wondered if she, too, was ill.

I felt her heart pounding,
her body pressed protectively
against me.

Or maybe it was mine.

I tried to tell her I was not pretending,
but with her arms wrapped
tightly around me,
I knew she knew I was not.

I wanted to tell her that
if Mrs. Dwyer should come
unexpectedly into the room,
she should tell her
I was not pretending.

I could hear the words
forming in my head,
but when I spoke them,
I could not hear them in my ears.

But it did not matter.

When I was buried,
Sarah
and Gracie
and Ruthie were there.

Miss Weston
and Mr. Davis were there.

Even Miss Prentiss was there.

But Mrs. Dwyer stayed in her room.

I wonder if Mrs. Dwyer thought
I was pretending
to be dead.

saraн

The days have passed, **WAIENHAWI.**
Ten days have passed.

I gave your notebook to Miss Weston.

I gave your combs to Gracie.

At each meal today,
I ate everything even though I was not hungry.

It was the best I could do, **WAIENHAWI.**

saraн

Mrs. Hunter watches over me while I work.
Waiting for me to do what?

I do not know.

I would like to think she cares about me,
that she cares that my sister is no longer.
But I think she only cares that I do my work.

And I will.

I will do my work and I will be good—for Mattie—
when it is right to be good.

I will do my work and I will be good—for me—
when it is right to be good.

I stand at the sink and scrub the spots clean.
The brush is coarse, and if I scrub too hard,
the bristles scrape against the side of my hand,
but I do not care.

I will do my work and be good—
when it is right to be good.

"Sarah," Mrs. Hunter shouts from across the room.
"Surely, you must be finished with that apron."

Her voice startles me so that my shoulders
jump upright and the brush flies out of my hand,
landing with a clunk on the stone floor.

"My goodness, child," she says with a sigh
so deep it says I make her tired.

I fix my face so that she cannot see my anger
and turn toward her in time to see her standing
with her hands on her hips and her head shaking
back and forth, back and forth, and I know
that she only cares about the work and not about me.

Or my sister.

AKTSI:'A

My older sister.

"I'm sorry," I tell her.

"Pick it up," she says insistently,
and I wonder if she thinks I would not think
to pick it up without her telling me so.

When she sees me bending down to retrieve
the brush that has slid in its soapiness under the sink,
she storms off toward Ruthie and the other girls
who have stopped to stare.

"Come, come, girls, back to work," she commands.

So much fuss over a silly brush,
Mattie would think.

So much fuss over cleaning clothes,
Mattie would think.

I often think now how Mattie would think.

On hands and knees, I crawl under the counter
that holds the metal sink and its iron drainpipes
that twist and turn underneath.

I reach for the brush, but as I wrap my fingers
around its wooden end, it slips away once more,
sliding even farther, and I find myself laughing
inside for the first time in many days,
laughing that a brush could be so mischievous,
finding its own stubborn way to avoid the work.

I think how Mattie would laugh out loud.

Life has returned, but to a brush.
It, too, does not want to work, scrubbing the spots
off an apron whose owner it does not know.

I creep farther into the darkness, wondering.
If I crawled far enough away,
would Mrs. Hunter wonder where I went?

I laugh again inside to think of Mrs. Hunter
crawling on her hands and knees under the sink
to look for me hiding in the darkness.

"Sarah," her voice barks above me.
"What are you doing under there?"

My laughter leaves.

"Looking for the brush," I tell her.
"It slipped away."

"Well, find it and get back to work."

"Yes, Mrs. Hunter."

I hear her rustling away.

I reach around behind the drainpipe
where the brush has slid and scoop it back
toward me without lifting it up,
and as the tips of my fingers brush against the pipe,
they are met with a sharp stab of pain.

"Ouch," I whisper to myself,
not wanting Mrs. Hunter to return.

I lean forward to suck the pain away
from my throbbing finger,
and as I bend my head downward,
a glint of metal catches my attention.

The pain in my finger stops instantly
and a pounding in my chest begins
and I cannot breathe, for the lack of air
in my throat makes me gasp and choke
and I dare not make a sound.

Mrs. Dwyer's pin stares at me.

Mrs. Dwyer's pin,
Mrs. Dwyer's ugly pin,
Mrs. Dwyer's ugly, dreadful pin,
only a few inches from my face.

My sister is saved.

But Mattie is gone, and there is no saving her anymore.

I snatch the pin and clutch it to my chest.

What do I do?

What do I do?

What do I do?

I want to jump up and dance around the room
and run out the door and across the yard and shout,
*Look, look, everyone. Can you see? Can you see now
that my sister is not a thief?*

Everyone will know the truth.

Everyone.

But Mattie knew the truth.

And I knew the truth.

But Mrs. Dwyer will never see the truth.

Will she believe me?

Will she believe that her pin has been hiding
under the sink?

Will she think I put it there?

Will she think I put it there to protect my sister?

What do I do?

I should be good.

I should give Mrs. Dwyer her pin
and hope she can see the truth.

But Mrs. Dwyer would have her pin back,
and I still would not have Mattie.

I should be good.

But it is not the right time to be good.

"Sarah," Mrs. Hunter shouts,
"What are you doing?"

"I have it," I respond quickly.

With the pin in one hand
and the brush in the other,
I move slowly backward, the heels of my hands
and the toes of my shoes pressing into the stone,
toward the openness of the room, inch by inch,
my brain searching for a plan.

Just as the darkness begins to fade,
replaced by the dim light of the laundry,
my toes catch in the iron grate of the drain
which allows the water that splashes from the sinks
and tubs to flow into the earth below.

My decision is made.

As I lift the found brush into the air
for Mrs. Hunter and all to see,
my left hand slides smoothly over the grate,
and as I unclench my fist, releasing the cause
of my sister's misery into the emptiness below,
I yell loud enough to cover any splash, any clink,
any thud that might occur.

"Here it is! I found it!"

saraн

"Come, come, let's line up," Ida commands
as we prepare to leave the dining hall
to return to our rooms after the evening meal.

I do not mind marching so much anymore.

I do not even mind Ida.

She has not looked at me since Mattie was buried.

But I look at her.

I look at everyone.

"Ready. March!" she calls out.

Mrs. Dwyer stands in the doorway,
nodding approvingly as we pass,
pleased with Ida in her new role as captain.

We are supposed to look straight ahead,
but I turn my head slightly and look at her,
directly into her black eyes.

She looks away.

Across the gravel drive and onto the pathway,
swinging our arms in unison, we stride,
Gracie in front and Ruthie behind,
the three of us in a long line of girls
marching to the dormitory.

Up the steps and into the main hall,
where the older girls file quickly into their rooms
while the rest of us continue on up to the second floor.

When we enter the long room, we break ranks.

Gracie goes directly to the box at the end of her bed
to collect her books and paper for study time,
but Ruthie tugs at my sleeve.

"Bring your speller," she says. "I need help."

Gracie and Ruthie and I now sit together
to do our lessons, helping one another
the way Mattie would help me.

"I will," I tell her. "Go ahead."

When I turn toward my own place in the room,
I am surprised by the presence of Mr. Davis.

We often see him working in and around our building,
fixing, cleaning, sweeping, but never so late.

"Evenin', Miss Sarah," he says,
giving me a nod and a slight smile.
"I's fixed dat bottom drawer fuh you."

His words confuse me.

He fixed my bureau long ago.
He fixed a handle, not a drawer.

"It took a little work," he says seriously.

"But it should be jus' fine now," he adds
as he heads out the door and into the hall.
"Everything'll be jus' fine."

I stare at this man, this man who is my friend,
this man who was my friend when all seemed lost,
this man who now confuses me.

He vanishes down the hall and, for a moment,
I continue to stare at the empty space.

I look at my bureau.

There was nothing wrong with my bureau,
nothing wrong with my bottom drawer.

I walk slowly to my bureau and stand before it,
running my fingers back and forth across the top.

I can feel my heart pulsing in my head,
but it is not fear, only confusion.

I tell myself I am not afraid.

I am not going to be afraid ever again.

Not of anything.

Not of anyone.

"Sarah? You coming?" Gracie asks,
standing in the doorway, waiting for me
to go with her and Ruthie to the study room.

"Go ahead," I tell her. "I will be there soon."

I wait until the room has emptied.

It is so quiet I hear only my own breathing.

I kneel down onto the wooden floor
and gently pull open the bottom drawer,
which slides out easily.

The scarf my mother made lies folded neatly,
and though I had no reason to worry,
a wave of relief rushes through me.

It is there.

Why should it not be?

I reach into the drawer to pat my scarf lovingly,
feeling somewhat silly at my concern for its safety,
feeling ashamed that perhaps I had thought
Mr. Davis's intrusion into my bureau
might have meant my most valued possession
was in some danger, and as my fingers touch
the softness of the wool, I feel a stiffness underneath.

In the quiet emptiness of the room,
I hear my breath rushing in and out,
making short gasping sounds as I search for air.

I pull the scarf out quickly and clutch it to my heart,
and though I promised Mattie I would never cry again,
I cannot stop the tears from flowing.

There, tucked in among my nightclothes,
there under the scarf my mother made with love for me,
was Mattie's gift from her.

Mattie's beautiful basket.

Mattie's beautiful sweetgrass basket.

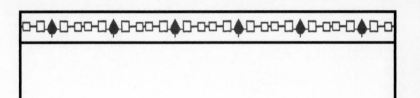

The **Ayonwatha** (Hiawatha) belt that appears
in the design of this book was the first wampum belt
made to commemorate the peaceful alliance of
the **Haudenosaunee** (Iroquois) nations.
It portrays the unity of the original five tribes and
represents the path of peace on which other nations
are welcome to travel, taking shelter beneath the
Great Tree of Peace.

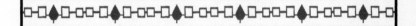